W9-BSH-885

Dawn and the Older Boy

Look for these and other books in the Baby-sitters Club series:

1 *Kristy's Great Idea*
2 *Claudia and the Phantom Phone Calls*
3 *The Truth About Stacey*
4 *Mary Anne Saves the Day*
5 *Dawn and the Impossible Three*
6 *Kristy's Big Day*
7 *Claudia and Mean Janine*
8 *Boy-Crazy Stacey*
9 *The Ghost at Dawn's House*
#10 *Logan Likes Mary Anne!*
#11 *Kristy and the Snobs*
#12 *Claudia and the New Girl*
#13 *Good-bye Stacey, Good-bye*
#14 *Hello, Mallory*
#15 *Little Miss Stoneybrook . . . and Dawn*
#16 *Jessi's Secret Language*
#17 *Mary Anne's Bad-Luck Mystery*
#18 *Stacey's Mistake*
#19 *Claudia and the Bad Joke*
#20 *Kristy and the Walking Disaster*
#21 *Mallory and the Trouble With Twins*
#22 *Jessi Ramsey, Pet-sitter*
#23 *Dawn on the Coast*
#24 *Kristy and the Mother's Day Surprise*
#25 *Mary Anne and the Search for Tigger*
#26 *Claudia and the Sad Good-bye*
#27 *Jessi and the Superbrat*
#28 *Welcome Back, Stacey!*
#29 *Mallory and the Mystery Diary*
#30 *Mary Anne and the Great Romance*
#31 *Dawn's Wicked Stepsister*
#32 *Kristy and the Secret of Susan*
#33 *Claudia and the Great Search*
#34 *Mary Anne and Too Many Boys*
#35 *Stacey and the Mystery of Stoneybrook*
#36 *Jessi's Baby-sitter*
#37 *Dawn and the Older Boy*
#38 *Kristy's Mystery Admirer*

Super Specials:

1 *Baby-sitters on Board!*
2 *Baby-sitters' Summer Vacation*
3 *Baby-sitters' Winter Vacation*
4 *Baby-sitters' Island Adventure*

Dawn and the Older Boy

Ann M. Martin

AN
APPLE
PAPERBACK

SCHOLASTIC INC.
New York Toronto London Auckland Sydney

Cover art by Hodges Soileau

No part of this publication may be reproduced in whole or in part, or stored in a retrieval system, or transmitted in any form or by any means, electronic, mechanical, photocopying, recording, or otherwise, without written permission of the publisher. For information regarding permission, write to Scholastic Inc., 730 Broadway, New York, NY 10003.

ISBN 0-590-43566-3

Copyright © 1990 by Ann M. Martin. All rights reserved. Published by Scholastic Inc. APPLE PAPERBACKS and THE BABY-SITTERS CLUB are registered trademarks of Scholastic Inc.

12 11 10 9 8 7 6 5 4 3 2 1 0 1 2 3 4 5/9

Printed in the U.S.A. 40

First Scholastic printing, September 1990

The author gratefully acknowledges
Mary Lou Kennedy
for her help in
preparing this manuscript.

Dawn and the Older Boy

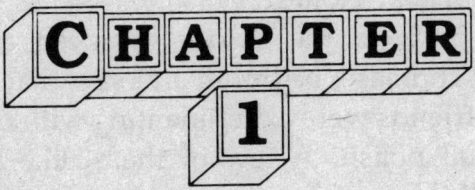

"I don't think orange is your color," Claudia Kishi said thoughtfully. "You're more the peaches-and-cream type, with your light skin and blonde hair."

"Mmm, I think you're right." I stared at myself in the mirror and reached for a tissue. The orange lipstick had to go. I looked like I had just kissed a pumpkin.

"Try this," Claudia went on, handing me a tube of gooey pink lip gloss. It reminded me of used bubble gum.

Claudia caught the expression on my face and burst out laughing. "Trust me, Dawn. It will be fantastic on you."

Claudia is an artist and can see shapes and colors in a way that nobody else can. It's a good thing that Claudia is creative because she's not the world's best student. (She's an especially bad speller.) And just to make things worse, she has this incredibly brainy older sister named Janine. Janine is the type of girl who sits around doing quadratic equations for *fun*. Honest.

But back to the story. I glanced around Kristy Thomas's bedroom and saw that all six of my friends were experimenting with lipstick and nail polish. A few of them, like Stacey McGill, were even trying out new hairstyles. It was a sort of mass "make-over," and there was a lot of giggling going on. (And some of the "befores" looked better than the "afters," if you know what I mean.)

I guess I should stop right here and introduce everybody before I tell you anything else about the sleepover at Kristy's. First of all, the seven of us are members of the Baby-sitters Club (or BSC), which I'll explain about later. My name is Dawn Schafer, and I am the alternate officer of the club. I live in Stoneybrook, Connecticut, and I am thirteen years old. My friends all say I *look* like a California girl with my *long* blonde hair and sparkly blue eyes. This makes sense since I lived in California before my parents got divorced and my mom and my brother Jeff and I moved to Stoneybrook. Now Jeff lives in California again with my father (he just wasn't happy in Connecticut), and sometimes I go back to visit. What else would you like to know? Well, I love the outdoors, I'm a vegetarian, and I try to eat a healthy diet. (Unlike Claudia, who thinks Gummi Bears are nature's perfect food.)

Claudia is a beautiful, dramatic-looking Japanese-American who loves exotic clothes. (She's also the vice-president of the BSC.) Claudia's one of those people who can wear anything and get away with it. Today, for example, she had stuck to two colors: black and white. Black cotton bib overalls over a white turtleneck with a shiny black patent leather belt looped around her waist. Black suede ankle boots and white cotton socks. Long black hair swept off her face with giant white plastic barrettes. Anyone else would look like a penguin in that get-up, but Claudia looked great.

"What do you think?" she asked, holding up a white hoop earring next to her face. "Too much?"

I nodded. "Maybe just a little." The earring was the size of a doorknob.

"Hey, Dawn, will you take a look at my hair?" asked Mary Anne. Mary Anne Spier is my stepsister (my mother married Richard, her father) and she is also my best friend. Mary Anne is a lot less daring with clothes and makeup than I am, but she has grown up quite a bit in the past year.

When I first met Mary Anne, she looked like a little girl. She was wearing little-girl clothes and, worst of all, she was wearing her brown hair in two long pigtails. Awful! When I got to know her better, I realized that she's really sweet and very sensitive, and that she dressed that way because her father picked out her clothes. See, Mary Anne's mother died when Mary Anne was just a baby, so her father has always been very protective of her. Luckily, he's loosened up a lot since he married my mom, and Mary Anne looks like a regular thirteen-year-old now. And she even has a steady boyfriend. She's the only one of us BSC members who can make that claim. Her boyfriend is named Logan Bruno, and he's part of the club, too. Mary Anne is the club secretary.

"What's the problem?" I asked, scooting over to her side of the room. The minute the words were out of my mouth, I knew the answer.

Stacey McGill (a real New York girl) was busily "scrunching" Mary Anne's long brown hair into a tangled mane that trailed down her back. Very hip, very in, but not very "Mary

Anne." I thought it looked fantastic, but I knew that Mary Anne was unhappy with it. Mary Anne usually wears her hair in a smooth style; she's used to seeing herself in a certain way. (I should explain that Mary Anne would never complain to Stacey, because she doesn't like to hurt anyone's feelings.)

"Honestly, Mary Anne, if you'd just keep your hands out of the way, this would go a lot quicker." Stacey had scrunched her own hair into a cloud of blonde curls and was trying for the same effect with my stepsister.

Mary Anne shot me a desperate look in the mirror, just as Stacey gave a final pat to her hair and said pointedly, "Doesn't she look great?"

I was on the spot. "I think it's a nice change," I began. "Of course, you wouldn't have to wear it that way every day."

"She should. It's a big improvement," Stacey said flatly. Stacey McGill, the club treasurer, is very fashion-conscious and always wears the newest, trendiest clothes. She is sophisticated, like Claudia (who happens to be her best friend), and she has boyfriends sometimes, but no steady ones. She's an only child and grew up in New York City until her father's company transferred him to Connecticut. The McGills had lived in Stoneybrook for a year when her father was sent *back* to New York. We all said tearful good-byes to Stacey and wondered if we would ever see her again. About a year later, Stacey's parents got divorced, and Stacey and her mom returned to Connecticut. Talk about a complicated life! Stacey still seems like a New York girl at heart (just like I am a California girl at heart) and she visits her father in New York whenever she can.

Just to add to Stacey's problems, she has a severe form of diabetes. She's very careful about what she eats and knows how to give herself insulin shots every day. Diabetes is something she has to live with, but at least she can keep it under control. The main thing she has to remember is not to eat sweets. Just imagine a life without sugar and candy, and you'll get the idea. At first, we tried not to have cookies or things lying around where she could see them, but we found out that Stacey has a lot of self-control. She doesn't eat those things because she knows she could get really sick.

"Well, it's finished," Stacey said. She put down the brush and reached for an apple. The rest of us were munching on fudge (except for me — too unhealthy), but that's off-limits for Stacey, of course.

"I appreciate it, I really do," Mary Anne said earnestly. I knew that Mary Anne would never wear her hair that way again, but she managed to look as if she were thrilled with her new style.

"I'll be glad to do it for you anytime," Stacey said. "The thing to remember is to use just a little bit of gel and — " She stopped talking suddenly and sat down on Kristy's bed.

"Are you okay?" Kristy Thomas asked. (Kristy Thomas is the president of the Baby-sitters Club, and she is a take-charge sort of person.)

"I'm fine," Stacey said lightly. She put her hand up to her forehead, just for a second, as though she had a headache.

"You look a little pale," Kristy said, peering at her. I remembered that Stacey hadn't felt well for the past few days.

"Hey, I'm fine. Really." Stacey bounced right back on her feet and picked up her styling brush. "I think I got a little dizzy from all the hairspray," she said with a smile. "Maybe we should get some air in here."

"Good idea." As usual, Kristy took command of the situation and marched over to the nearest window. Sometimes I get a little annoyed because Kristy tends to be bossy (wait till you see her at a club meeting, and you'll understand), but I have to admit she really gets things done. It's funny, because in some ways, Kristy seems a little younger than thirteen. She has zero interest in clothes and makeup and practically lives in her favorite outfit: a turtleneck, faded jeans, and running shoes. But in other ways, she seems very mature and is exactly the kind of person you would want to have around in an emergency.

Kristy has an interesting family. She has three brothers — Sam and Charlie, who are in high school, and David Michael, who's only seven. For a long time, Mrs. Thomas supported the family all by herself, because her husband had walked out one day and never come back. It was very hard on everyone, but Mrs. Thomas managed to get a good job and keep the family together. Then (and this is the wonderful part) she met a millionaire named Watson Brewer and they married and the Thomases moved across town into his mansion! It sounds like something out of a movie, doesn't it? Watson Brewer has two children, Karen, who has just turned seven, and Andrew, who's four, so Kristy found herself with a new brother and sister. (They only live with their father every other weekend and for two weeks during the summer, though.) Things got even *more* interesting after that because the Brewers adopted an adorable little Vietnamese girl whom they named Emily. By now Kristy's family was beginning to look like the Brady Bunch, so Nannie, Kristy's grandmother, moved in to help. Kristy loves her new family, and since she's terrific with kids, she's a big help with her younger brothers and sisters.

Okay, now I need to tell you about the two junior officers of the BSC, Mallory Pike and Jessica Ramsey. While the rest of us are eighth-graders at Stoneybrook Middle School, they are eleven and in sixth grade at SMS. They are very different, but they are best friends.

Actually, Mal and Jessi have a couple of things in common. They are both the oldest in their families (that can have some good points and some bad points). And they share some interests.

Let's start with Mal. Mal comes from an *enormous* family. She has seven brothers and sisters, including a set of identical triplets (boys). Mallory is very creative and loves to read and write and draw. Her dream in life is to write and illustrate children's books, and I think she would do a wonderful job.

Jessi has an eight-year-old sister named Becca (short for Rebecca) and a baby brother named Squirt. Squirt? That's right. His real name is John Philip Ramsey, Jr., but he was so tiny when he was born that the nurses in the hospital nicknamed him Squirt.

Jessi also likes to read (she and Mal both love horse stories), but her real talent is quite different from Mallory's. Jessi wants to be a professional dancer and has studied ballet for years. It takes a lot of skill and hard work to get roles in major ballets and to perform in front of hundreds of people, but Jessi has what it takes. She doesn't even get stage fright. (I know I would faint dead away if I had to do something like that.)

One other difference between Jessi and Mal — Jessi is black and Mal is white.

I have a lot more things I want to tell you about my friends (especially about my stepsister, Mary Anne, and the really romantic way our parents got together), but I will have to save that for later. Stay tuned!

At eleven o'clock the following morning, Mary Anne tapped me on the shoulder.

"Dawn, wake up," she said urgently. "It's practically lunchtime!"

I snuggled deeper into my sleeping bag and buried my face in the pillow. "Uh-huh," I mumbled. What was Mary Anne getting all steamed up about? *Nobody* bounces out of bed the morning after a sleepover, and besides, we hadn't turned out the lights till three A.M. No wonder I felt like a zombie.

But Mary Anne wouldn't give up. She sat down next to me. "I think we should all get up right this minute," she said firmly. "We've already wasted half the day!"

"Quit talking," Stacey muttered from her sleeping bag. "Some people are trying to sleep."

"I know you are," Mary Anne apologized.

"But I think the Brewers expect us to show up for breakfast. We shouldn't be lounging around in bed all morning when they're trying to feed sixteen in the kitchen." I hated to admit it, but I decided Mary Anne was probably right. I also thought that my stepsister was the only person in the whole world who would worry about something like that.

"Mmm, I think I smell bacon cooking," Mal said. She wriggled off her air mattress and stretched. "I agree with Mary Anne. We should all go downstairs."

Jessi gave a gigantic yawn. "I've decided to have breakfast in bed," she said sleepily. "Just leave a tray outside the door for me."

"Ha! Fat chance!" Claudia yelled, tossing a pillow at her. "If we get up, *you* get up."

Mary Anne yanked open the drapes, and the room was flooded with harsh yellow sunlight. Everybody *really* woke up after that, including Kristy, who had burrowed like a mole under her fluffy pink quilt.

"Hey, Kristy," Stacey asked, "do we have to get dressed to go down to breakfast?"

"On a Saturday morning? Are you kidding?" Kristy grinned and jammed her feet into a pair of fat down slippers. "That's the great part about weekends. You can wear whatever you want, and Mom and Watson won't care. Honest."

Claudia glanced in the mirror. Her hair was a mass of tangles and her mascara had smudged over her cheekbones in two dark shadows. She looked like someone straight out of *Night of the Living Dead.*

"Claudia, you look awful," Kristy said cheerfully.

"You don't look so terrific yourself," Claudia retorted. She wasn't in the least bit offended because the truth is we *all* looked awful.

"I know. Isn't it fun?" Kristy grabbed her favorite baseball cap (the one with the collie on it) and plunked it on her head. "But who's going to see us at breakfast except for Karen and Nannie and Mom and everyone?"

A few minutes later we had our answer. Who was going to see us? Only the cutest guy in the whole world!

Talk about having a panic attack. All seven of us had trooped downstairs, looking our absolute worst, when we realized there were *boys* sitting around the kitchen table! Two of them were Kristy's older brothers, Charlie and Sam, and the other looked like a movie star. Sandy brown hair, deep blue eyes, and a smile that

I knew I would never forget. Claudia was in front of me, and she skidded to a stop just like the Road Runner in that Saturday morning cartoon show. Naturally, I bumped into her, and she lurched against the back of Sam's chair.

"Oh, Claudia. Hi there." He glanced at Kristy. "I figured you were going to sleep all day." Sam took a quick peek at the rest of us, and his jaw dropped open. Why hadn't we taken a few extra minutes to brush our hair and put on a little makeup? (Or at least take off the old makeup?) I know I looked terrible. I have very light skin and, as I've said, my hair is so blonde it's practically white. Can you imagine what I look like first thing in the morning, especially with mascara smudges under my eyes?

I tried to duck behind Stacey, who immediately caught on and started inching her way back toward the hallway.

"Hey, don't run away," Charlie teased her. "Kristy, I want you and your friends to meet someone." He waved a hand at the fantastic-looking boy at the table. "Travis, meet my sister and the rest of the Baby-sitters Club. Travis just moved to Stoneybrook," he went on.

Travis half rose out of his chair and smiled at everyone. (He could afford to be cheerful. He looked terrific, and the rest of us were wrecks.) The other kids in the family were at the table with him. Emily was spooning up cornflakes with David Michael, Karen, and Andrew, but I barely looked at them. I couldn't take my eyes off Travis (and I couldn't stop wishing I were invisible)! Why did I have to look my absolute worst?

Travis was too polite to look shocked, though, and I thought I would drop through the floor when he reached across the table and shook my hand! No one my age shakes hands (do they?), but somehow it seemed just right when Travis did it.

I could feel a little ripple of excitement go through the group, even though most of us were busily staring at our toes and wishing we were on another planet. There was this incredibly long silence while everyone waited for someone else to think of something to say, and Travis and I just stood and stared at each other.

Without thinking, I blurted out the first words that came into my head. "Is that granola you're eating?" Not the brightest remark in the world, but you have to realize that this was a crisis situation. Think how you would feel if you happened to be wearing a tattered old nightgown and a three-sizes-too-big terry robe at a time like this. It was enough to make anyone tongue-tied.

"That's right," Travis said easily. "It's practically the state food in California." *He was from California!* "Why don't you join us?" He gestured to an empty seat beside him, and it was all I could do not to throw myself into it. Then I remembered my shiny face (and morning breath) and decided against it.

"Oh, we'll get something to eat later," I said, trying to sound totally cool and in command of the situation. (I wasn't in control at all, and my heart was beating like a rabbit's.)

"Breakfast is the most important meal of the day," he said teasingly.

"I know that," I replied, nodding. If he wanted to talk nutrition, that was fine with me. Mom and I are fanatics about eating healthy food, and we even make our own breakfast cereal.

Kristy, as usual, took charge. "I really think we should be heading back upstairs," she said firmly.

"Yeah, that's right." Claudia was stepping sideways toward the door.

"Without having breakfast?" Sam said, looking amused, as if he knew exactly what we were up to.

Claudia shrugged and pushed her long black hair out of her face. "Well, actually, we . . . uh, left our electric curlers switched on in the bathroom."

"Oh, that's right," Mary Anne piped up. (I should tell you that Mary Anne is a *terrible* liar.) "Gee," she added, "if we don't get back upstairs right away, the curlers might overheat and burn the house down." Charlie snickered and even Travis looked a little amused.

Without another word, all seven of us stampeded toward the door. I had time for one last look at Travis, and when his blue eyes zeroed in on mine, I felt a funny little flutter in my chest.

Upstairs, I took a quick shower and spent the next hour fiddling with my hair and makeup. I decided that I wanted to look casual (but gorgeous!) and finally settled on a pale blue ten-button top with my favorite jeans. (Not that I had much choice, since I'd only packed for an overnight.)

When we went back downstairs it was almost twelve o'clock, and guess what. The boys were still there! I couldn't believe my luck. I made *sure* that Travis noticed me and slid onto the bench next to him.

"You must be starving," he said, pushing a bowl of fruit toward me.

"Ravenous," I replied, taking a tiny bite of an apple. Who could think about food at a time like this?

"Hey, Travis," Charlie spoke up, "did I mention that you and Dawn have something in common? She's from California, too."

"Really? That's fantastic." Travis looked like he had been waiting all his life for this bit of information. "Do you miss the ocean? We lived right on the ocean, and I used to go for long walks on the beach every night after dinner."

"You *did?* We didn't live on the ocean, but I used to take long walks, too." I was so excited I nearly dropped my apple. Have you ever met someone and felt like you've always known that person? That was the way I felt about Travis.

"There's a place just above Malibu," Travis began, "and when the sun sets, it looks like it's dropping right into the ocean."

"I know. I went there once." I felt almost giddy. Travis and I talked nonstop for the next half hour and I have *never* met anyone whose feelings were so close to my own. We could have been twins.

"You know, you should always wear blue," Travis said, gently touching my sleeve. "It brings out the color of your eyes. Just like the ocean. . . ."

What an unbelievable morning! I couldn't get Travis off my mind for the rest of the day, and I practically drove Mary Anne crazy talking about him.

"Mary Anne, do you believe in love at first sight?" I asked her the minute we were back home.

"I think so," she said slowly. "Look at your father and my mother. I think they fell in love at first sight in high school. It's just that it took them all this time to get together."

Remember that romantic story I promised to tell you about our parents? This is it. My mom dated Mary Anne's father in high school (we didn't know this when I first moved to Stoneybrook) and they went steady. They were madly in love with each other — but now comes the sad part. My grandparents (my mom's mother and father) disapproved of Mary Anne's father and didn't want my mom to keep dating him. Why? Because he didn't have a lot of money. My mom comes from a wealthy family, and I guess they always thought she would marry someone rich. I'm glad to say that the story has a happy ending. My mom and Richard *did* find each other again (with a little help from Mary Anne and me), and now they are happily married and we all live in my house.

I had to ask another question. "Mary Anne," I said, "what did you think of Travis? Don't you think he's the most gorgeous boy you've ever seen?"

"Travis?" She looked at me suspiciously. "Dawn, you're not going to get some kind of hopeless crush on him, are you?"

A hopeless crush! I was insulted. "Of course not," I said stiffly. "I just think he's very . . . attractive."

"Oh, well, sure," Mary Anne said. "I do, too. Of course, *I* think *Logan* is gorgeous." She paused. Mary Anne and I know each other so well that she could guess what I was thinking. "Dawn," she said, "I just want to remind you that he's in *high* school. . . ."

"I know that."

"And that even if *you* like *him,* it doesn't

mean he's going to ask you out or anything."

"Right." I changed the subject then, but my mind kept racing along the same channels. I had found the one boy in the world for me, and his name was Travis.

A lot of kids hate Monday, but I don't mind it. Why? Because Monday is the first meeting day of the week for the Baby-sitters Club. I know you're probably wondering about the club and how it works, so I'm going to fill you in on our last meeting. It took place the Monday after the sleepover, and if you're guessing that I was still thinking about Travis, you're absolutely right.

I should begin by telling you that we meet on Mondays, Wednesdays, and Fridays, and that we start *promptly* at five-thirty. And that means on the dot! Kristy Thomas, our president, is a stickler for being on time (and for a lot of other rules as well). We meet for half an hour, until six o'clock.

I scooted into Claudia's bedroom about two minutes late (due to a sitting job), and got an icy glare from Kristy. She was sitting in her director's chair, as usual, and made a big production out of looking at Claud's digital clock, the official BSC timepiece. She didn't say anything, but she gave her head a little shake, and I knew she was annoyed.

"Sorry," I said, stepping between Mallory and Jessi, and settling myself on Claud's bed between Claud and Mary Anne. Mal and Jessi were smiling at each other, and I knew that they were trying not to giggle at some private joke. Since they're a couple of years younger than the rest of us, you would think that Kristy would bend the rules a little for them. No way! Whoever said rules are made to be broken never met Kristy Thomas.

You're probably curious about why we meet in Claudia's bedroom. That's easy — Claudia is the only one of us with her own phone and personal phone number. And a phone is very important when you're running an organization like the BSC. Why did I call it an organization? Because it's partly a club and partly a business.

Maybe I better back up and tell you how it got started. One day, before Kristy's mother had married Watson, when Kristy still lived across the street from Claudia and next door to Mary Anne, she noticed that her mother was calling all over town, trying to find a baby-sitter for David Michael, Kristy's little brother. Kristy got a brainstorm. Why not form a baby-sitters club — an organization that parents could call to reach several sitters at once.

This is the way our club works. My friends and I meet three times a week, as I mentioned, and anyone who wants a baby-sitter can call us at those times — and reach *seven* sitters. It's wonderful for the parents and great for us. We sometimes have more jobs than we can handle (which is why we have a couple of backup baby-sitters), and everything is done on a very professional basis.

We have elected officers, we collect dues, and we keep very accurate records of who sits when and how much money they make. We also write down our baby-sitting "experiences" in a notebook. This information is very helpful to all the club members and gives us tips about what to expect from the kids.

You already know that Kristy Thomas is the president, and I would say that she is perfect for the job. Even though she does tend to be a little bit bossy, I have to admit that she keeps the club running well. (Plus, let's face it. I can't really think of anyone else in the club who would want to be president. It's a *lot* of responsibility. Besides, the club was Kristy's idea.)

Claudia Kishi is our vice-president because we felt it was only fair since we use her room three times a week, tie up her phone, and eat her junk food.

Mary Anne is the secretary, and she keeps the record book in good shape. Don't get confused. The record book is different from the notebook. The record book is like a giant appointment book. Mary Anne schedules every single baby-sitting job, and since she is very good at details, she actually *enjoys* doing this. She also keeps track of clients' names, addresses, and phone numbers, and the rates our clients pay. Mary Anne could tell you anything about our schedules — the date of Jessi's next dance class, or when Mal is due to have her braces checked. Mary Anne *never* makes mistakes, and as far as I know, has never mixed up a baby-sitting appointment. Mary Anne's job would drive me straight up the wall, but she loves it.

Stacey McGill is the club treasurer because she's practically a genius with numbers. She keeps track of who makes what (each of us keeps the money we make, though; we don't split it with the group), but it's good to know how things stand. Stacey is also responsible for collecting dues from everyone each Monday. The dues are pretty low, and the money is well spent, but it's still hard to get people to part with money. Actually, the dues are important for several reasons. We help Claudia pay her phone bill, and we pay Charlie, Kristy's oldest brother, to drive her to and from the meetings, since she lives in a different neighborhood, now that her mother has married Watson. We also use the money to restock our Kid-Kits (I'll explain later), and if there is any money left over, we blow it on fun things like pizza parties.

Not to be snide or anything, but as alternate officer, I think I have the most interesting job in the BSC. I get to fill in for any club member who can't make it to the meeting. Since Kristy is such a stickler for attendance, that hardly ever happens, but I've been the vice-president and the secretary, and I was club treasurer while Stacey was back in New York. I like being able to try all different jobs.

Mal and Jessi are our junior officers because they're not allowed to baby-sit at night yet, unless they're sitting for their own brothers and sisters. Still, they are both *very* responsible and are a big help to us in the club by taking on a lot of the after-school jobs.

Finally, we have two associate members, Shannon Kilbourne and Logan Bruno — Mary Anne's boyfriend! Shannon and Logan don't come to our regular meetings, but we know we can call on them in a pinch when we really get swamped with jobs. They are both good baby-sitters.

Anyway, back to the meeting. We were discussing club business, but my mind was filled with Travis. I was *dying* to ask Kristy if she had seen him again, but I couldn't think of any way to work it into the conversation.

Kristy must have noticed that I was a million miles away because she said suddenly, "How about you, Dawn? Do you need some more crayons or Magic Markers for your Kid-Kit?"

It took me a minute to come back to earth. "Uh, no, but I'd like to buy a few more coloring books."

This is what a Kid-Kit is. We each made our own. It's a decorated cardboard box filled with our old toys, books, and games, and we take it with us when we baby-sit. The kids love them, and the kits are part of what makes our club so special. For some reason, someone else's old toys are much more interesting than your own. However, although the toys and games last forever, certain items, like crayons and coloring books, need to be replaced from time to time. We use money from the treasury for this.

My mind was racing, though, trying to fit Travis into the conversation, and a minute later, I got my chance. Kristy mentioned that Charlie would be a little late picking her up at Claudia's.

"Oh, really? Is he out somewhere with Travis?" I asked, trying to sound ultracasual.

Kristy gave me a funny look. "No, he's at the dentist getting a cavity filled."

"Gee, that doesn't sound like much fun." I tried to laugh, but it didn't quite come off. "So how's he doing, anyway?" I asked.

Kristy rolled her eyes. "I'm sure he's fine. It was a very small cavity. Now if we can get back to business . . ."

"I don't mean Charlie," I said quickly. "I mean Travis." *Everybody* was looking at me now, and I knew I was probably giving the whole thing away by being so persistent.

Kristy shrugged. "How should I know?" She glanced down at the notebook, all set to talk about Charlotte Johanssen, who is one of our favorite sitting charges.

"You mean Travis hasn't been back to your house?" The words just tumbled out.

Kristy looked at me suspiciously. "Maybe once or twice," she said vaguely. "I think he came over to shoot some baskets yesterday."

"You *think?*" How could she not know a thing like that?

"There were a lot of boys playing basketball in the driveway," she snapped. "Now we really need to . . ."

I tuned out the rest of what Kristy was saying. Item one: Travis may or may not have been back to her house. Item two: Travis *probably* hadn't mentioned me, at least not to Kristy. (But maybe to one of her brothers? I couldn't be sure.) I really hadn't found out very much in this conversation, but at least it was fun to talk about Travis. I just liked hearing his name!

The phone rang just then, and Kristy grabbed it. "Good afternoon, Baby-sitters Club." Kristy listened for a few moments, jotted down some notes, and promised to get back to the caller. I should explain that everyone is "equal" in our club. Just because you answer the phone doesn't mean you can take the job for yourself (although this has happened a few times). Instead, you are supposed to write down the details of the job, discuss it with the club members, let Mary Anne check the record book, and *then* call the client back. It's a good system.

"That was Mrs. Hobart," Kristy said, looking around the group. "She needs a sitter for Johnny, Mathew, and James next Saturday because Ben is taking Mal to the movies."

Six of us gasped, and Mal turned an interesting shade of pink.

"Is that true?" I asked. "You and Ben are going out together?" I should mention that the Hobarts are an Australian family who moved into Mary Anne's old house across the street. There are four boys in the family, all with reddish-gold hair and "Aussie" accents. Ben Hobart, the oldest in the family, is Mal's age and a really nice boy.

"I wouldn't call it going out together," Mal said. She looked a little flustered, and I knew she wasn't thrilled at being the center of attention. "We're just going to a movie."

"Sounds like going out to me," I teased her. Naturally, my mind went to Travis. I'd give *anything* to go to a movie with him, and I wouldn't care if anyone called it going out or not.

"Let's get back to business," Kristy said crisply. "Who's available on Saturday?" Mary Anne pored through the record book, and it turned out that Jessi was free.

She nodded to Kristy, who already had her hand on the phone. "Tell her I'll be there," Jessi piped up. "The Hobarts are great."

The meeting broke up shortly after that, and Mary Anne and I rode our bikes home in the fading sunlight. I couldn't help but think about Mal and her date-that-wasn't-really-a-date. I tried to imagine what it would be like to go on a date with Travis. What if he just called me up out of the blue and asked me out? What if he asked me out for pizza or a movie? What would I do, what would I say, what would I wear? I was thinking so hard, I nearly rode into the gutter.

"Dawn, wake up!" Mary Anne said. "You're in another world."

I tightened my grip on the handlebars and tried to look serious. It was hard, though, because I really *was* in another world. A world filled with just two people — myself and Travis.

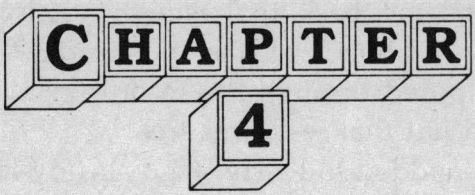

Have you ever had a funny feeling that something exciting was going to happen to you? That's how I felt during the next few days, except I wasn't sure if it was going to be wonderful-exciting or awful-exciting. (Once I just *knew* that I was going to have an exciting day, and that was the day Claudia broke her leg. So it's better not to get your hopes up too high when that feeling hits you.)

The feeling was pretty strong by the weekend, though. At about ten o'clock on a sunny Saturday morning, Mary Anne and I were raking the front yard while our parents were out shopping. We have a really *enormous* lawn, and when it's covered with leaves, it seems as big as a football field. But before you picture the yard, I better tell you about our house. When Mom and I moved to Stoneybrook after the divorce, we didn't buy a normal house like most people. Instead, we bought a colonial farmhouse that's over *two hundred* years old. I love it. It has lots of little rooms, and the doorways are so low that tall people have to duck under them. Mom says people used to be shorter in the 1700s. Anyway, it also has a smokehouse, a barn, and an *outhouse*. If you like spooky old houses, then you'd love this one, because it even has a secret passage. There's a long dark tunnel that leads from my bedroom to the barn, and we think that it was probably part of the Underground Railroad, which helped slaves escape from the South before and during the Civil War. It's exactly like something out of a ghost story. (I'm a big fan of ghost stories, in case you hadn't guessed.)

But back to that Saturday morning. Mary Anne and I had gotten up early and pulled on our oldest jeans, ready to tackle the front yard. Even with two people raking, it was like attacking an iceberg with a toothpick, but we were making some progress. I was wearing my Walkman, lost in my own world, when Mary Anne grabbed me by the arm.

"Look, look!" she mouthed. She pushed me around so I faced the driveway, and my stomach did a somersault. A dark blue Chevy was pulling up in front of our house, and a moment later, a terrific-looking boy got out. Not just *any* terrific-looking boy, though. *Travis.*

"Ohmigosh!" I whispered to Mary Anne, pulling off my headphones. "What am I going to do?" I felt like someone had just yanked the lawn out from under my feet, and I nearly dropped the rake.

"You're going to say hello to him," Mary Anne said calmly. (It was easy for her to be calm, because she didn't feel the same way about him that I did.)

By now, Travis was strolling toward us, and without thinking, I brushed my hair out of my eyes. Unfortunately, I also left a big black smudge on my face, but I didn't realize it.

"What will I say? How do I look?" I asked desperately. Mary Anne smiled and didn't answer me. She was already waving hello to Travis and heading back toward the house. I know she was giving us the chance to talk privately (Mary Anne is *always* tactful), but suddenly, I didn't want her to leave. I was afraid to be alone with Travis, afraid that I would make an idiot out of myself. (Also, Richard and my mom have very strict rules about us having boys over when they are not home. Boys are not allowed in the house. Period.)

"Hi, there," Travis said, walking up to me. (He certainly wasn't nervous.) He looked fantastic in a pair of jeans faded to just the right blue-white shade, and a heavy, new SHS (Stoneybrook High School) jacket.

"I didn't know you could drive," I blurted out. What a brilliant remark. For some reason, whenever I was around Travis, I seemed to lose the power of reasonable speech.

He shrugged, not the least bit embarrassed. "I've been driving since the day I turned sixteen."

I should explain that it's legal to drive at sixteen in Connecticut, but I don't know anyone who really starts driving at that age. The parents of Charlie Thomas, and a lot of other kids I know, make them wait until they're *seventeen* before they can drive alone. Some parents even make their kids wait until they're seventeen just to take the driver's test.

"Um, I like your car." This wasn't the world's most fascinating remark, either, but it was the best I could do under the circumstances.

"Thanks." Travis looked pleased, and we

automatically started walking back toward the house. I waited about fifteen seconds for him to say something (it seemed like fifteen hours) and finally asked him if he'd like some lemonade.

"Maybe a little later," he said, turning on that thousand-kilowatt smile. "Why don't we sit out here and talk for awhile." He touched my elbow and gestured to the front step.

"Sure." I gulped. So Travis really *had* come over just to talk to me. You're probably wondering why I didn't know this all along. I guess I did, but I couldn't believe it. I nearly asked him what he wanted to talk about but caught myself just in time. I decided it was time to stop making stupid remarks and try to start a real conversation. Before I had a chance to open my mouth again, he beat me to it.

"Fifty thousand miles on her, but you'd never know it," he said, pointing to the Chevy.

I nodded, not sure how to respond. Was fifty thousand miles good or bad? It sounded like a *lot* of miles, but since I don't drive, I'm not really up on things like this. I decided to play it safe. "It's nice that your parents let you borrow it," I said.

Travis laughed. "Borrow it? She's all mine. I can drive her whenever I want." He paused and pulled out a package of sugarless gum. After offering me a stick (I refused — the last thing I wanted to do was get gum stuck to my teeth during an important conversation) he went on. "I have to pay for the gas and the insurance."

I nodded again. I was beginning to feel like one of those doll heads that bob up and down in the back windows of cars. "It looks very . . . shiny," I said finally.

Travis beamed and I knew I had said the right thing. "Three coats of Super-Gloss," he said proudly. "You see, Dawn, the whole trick is to dry the car thoroughly in between each coat. A lot of people don't take the time, and that's why they get water spots."

"Oh," I said appreciatively. I had never thought about water spots before, but Travis made them sound almost interesting. "I'll have to remember that."

"And always use an old terry cloth towel. It doesn't scratch the finish, but it gives you a nice shine. That's extremely important." I smiled and tried to look encouraging.

We could probably have talked about cars a

little more, but Travis abruptly changed the subject. "So tell me, how do you like Stoneybrook Middle School?"

"Oh, I think it's great," I began. "All my friends are there — "

"That's nice," he cut in. "I make friends easily, too. A lot of people think it's tough to change schools, but not for me. I make friends wherever I go."

"So I guess you like Stoneybrook High — "

"You bet!" Travis said enthusiastically. "The first day I was there, I was invited to join five clubs. Five!" He ticked them off on his fingers. "The debate club, the drama club, the pep club, the computer club . . . oh, yeah, and the Latin club."

"That's nice," I said weakly. The Latin club didn't surprise me a bit — I was pretty sure it was all girls.

"And once they found out I play soccer and tennis" (Travis shook his head in mock amazement) "they drafted me on the spot."

"Wow!" That was all I could manage before Travis revved up again. I had never met anyone so energetic. (Or so talented, or so good-looking . . .)

"It was really funny," he added, "but the next day, Coach Higgins and Coach Reilly both showed up at the same time. One wanted me for basketball and the other wanted me for football." He laughed. "It was like a tug-of-war."

"I can imagine." I laughed a little to show I was getting into the spirit of things.

"Well, that's enough about me," he said suddenly. "Let's talk about you." He pulled out a small white box. "I brought you something."

A present? I nearly fainted. Even my daydreams hadn't prepared me for this. "What is it?" I cried.

"Open it up and see." Travis grinned at me. "I think you're going to like it."

My first present from Travis. My hands were shaking as I untied the bow. "A necklace!" I lifted a string of beautiful blue beads out of the box.

"There's more," Travis said. I found two hair combs nestled in the tissue paper. They were deep blue, like the beads.

"But it's not my birthday or anything," I protested.

Travis leaned forward and gently lowered the necklace over my head. "When I saw this, it just made me think of you. That's all. It's the same shade as your eyes."

"It is?" I felt ridiculously pleased.

"Definitely. And I had a special reason for buying the combs. I saw a girl on TV who had her hair swept back at the sides, like this." He lifted my fine blonde hair and tucked it behind my ears. "This is a much better style for you. It brings out your eyes and your cheekbones. I think you should try it."

"I guess I could," I said, flustered. "Usually, I just brush my hair and wear it straight. It's so long."

"Oh, yeah. That's another thing I wanted to mention." Travis picked up a strand of hair and looked at it critically. "When's the last time you got your hair cut?"

"Cut? I never get it cut. Well, sometimes I have the ends trimmed a little."

Travis gave me a very serious look. "I think you should lose a few inches, maybe three or four. It will give your hair more lift, you know?"

"Maybe," I said doubtfully. I like my hair the way it is — very long and fine. Whenever I try a new style, I usually hate it and go right back to wearing it straight.

"I'm not talking about anything drastic," Travis went on, "just a sort of trim. You could just ask the hairdresser or someone to shape it up if you want." He laid his hand very gently over mine, just for second. "Think about it, okay? For me."

For me! I nearly slid off the step. I knew that Travis must be really interested in me or he never would have gone to all this trouble.

"Of course I will," I told him.

He grinned and stood up. "I've got to run. My mom wants me to go shopping for her."

"Thanks for the necklace and the combs — " I began awkwardly.

"That's okay," Travis interrupted, heading toward the car. "But remember, I want to see you in that new hairstyle." He started the engine, waved good-bye, and headed down the street.

I stood rooted to the spot with a silly grin on my face. Travis liked me!

I could have stood there daydreaming forever, but I didn't want to waste a minute. I picked up the combs and dashed inside the house.

"Mary Anne!" I yelled, thundering up the stairs. "Get a brush and some scissors. We have work to do!"

Saturday

I never know what to expect when I sit for the Hobarts, and this time I got an even bigger surprise than usual. The kids asked me to watch them rehearse a play! And guess what. James, who is only eight years old, wrote it all by himself. He made sure that everybody got a part, and Chewy, believe it or not, was the star! It was great! I'll tell you more about it at our next meeting.

Jessi's baby-sitting job with the Hobarts turned out to be one of the best afternoons of her life. Who would think that putting on a play with five kids (the three Hobart boys and two of the Perkins girls) could be so much fun?

When the Hobarts first moved into the neighborhood, naturally everyone was very curious about them. Some of the kids said that the Hobarts talked just like Crocodile Dundee, so we decided to see for ourselves. What did we find? Four boys, all with red hair and great accents! But a few kids actually *made fun* of the way the Hobarts talked, and we thought this was incredibly rude. After all, maybe the Hobarts thought *we* sounded funny with our American accents.

But back to Jessi's baby-sitting job. Mrs. Hobart asked her to come over at two o'clock on Saturday afternoon. She and her husband were going out shopping and they needed someone to watch the three youngest boys, James, age eight; Mathew, age six; and Johnny, who is only four. Ben, the oldest boy, is in my class, so he obviously didn't need a sitter. And anyway, he was taking Mal to the movies that afternoon.

The three younger boys were playing outside when Myriah and Gabbie Perkins ran over to say hello.

"Hi, Jessi Ramsey," Gabbie yelled. Gabbie is two and a half and calls most people by their full names. She has two sisters, Myriah, who is almost six, and Laura, who is just a baby. The Perkinses moved into Bradford Court when they bought Kristy's old house. They have given the BSC lots of business, and we love to sit for them.

All three girls are great, and Myriah is especially theatrical. She can sing and dance (tap *and* ballet), and is even into gymnastics. Since Jessi is a dancer, she feels that she has a lot in common with her. Jessi says she's always impressed when little kids can get up and perform, because she knows how hard it is to face an audience. Myriah can sing "On the Good Ship Lollipop," and she knows "Tomorrow" from *Annie* by heart. A lot of kids love to sing, but Myriah is really good at it. She's just like someone you'd see on TV. When she sings, she knows every word. She's right on pitch and she even gets the timing right.

Anyway, when the Perkins girls ran over, they didn't come alone. They brought their dog with them. Chewbacca is a huge black

Labrador who is extremely friendly. (Sometimes *too* friendly!) He looks like a small bear but acts like a puppy.

"Chewbacca, quit that!" Myriah shouted. Chewbacca was running in circles, trampling the Hobarts' flower beds. "He's just had a bath," she explained, "and that always makes him crazy."

"Bring him over to the patio," Jessi said. "Let's all sit at the picnic table and play a game."

"What kind of game?" Mathew asked. He still has a trace of an Australian accent. "Something fun?"

"Definitely something fun." Jessi looked at Chewbacca. Playing Frisbee was out. Chewbacca had already chomped his way through three of them.

"Let's have a rehearsal," Myriah suggested. "That's my favorite thing to do in the whole world."

"A rehearsal?" Jessi said blankly. "I was thinking of playing 'I Packed My Grandmother's Trunk' — " She was immediately outvoted.

"No, we want to rehearse!" James and Mathew yelled. "We'll show you our play." I should tell you that the Hobart kids are very interested in drama, and Mathew was given the lead in his school play.

"You're putting on a play?" Jessi asked.

"An original one," James said proudly. "I'm writing it."

An eight-year-old kid writing a play? Jessi was impressed.

"We've been working on it for a couple of weeks," Myriah piped up. "Do you want to see how far we've gotten?"

"Sure," Jessi told her. And she saw the perfect opportunity to send Chewbacca back to his own house. "But don't you think you better take Chewy home first? You could leave him on the sun porch so he won't interrupt the rehearsal."

"No, Chewbacca has to stay," Myriah replied. "Mommy says we have to keep him outside till he dries off." She grinned. "Besides, he's our star."

Oh, no. Jessi groaned inwardly. Then she poured herself a glass of lemonade and sat back to watch the show. After a few minutes, she found herself getting *really* interested. Even though there was a lot of giggling (and almost everyone forgot some of their lines), the play was good.

The story was very simple. Chewy (the hero) was a lost dog who wandered up and down a busy shopping mall, looking for his owner. Jessi started to point out that dogs aren't usually allowed in malls, but she knew that would spoil the fun.

Myriah had the opening lines. "Hello, doggie," she said brightly. "Don't you have a home?" She walked up to Chewy and pretended to inspect his neck. "Uh-oh," she said, making a face. "No collar." She rolled her eyes. "Now it's going to be really hard to find your owner." Chewy jumped up and started licking her face. "Down, Chewy," she said sharply. "I mean, down, doggie."

Gabbie cleared her throat, eager to get into the act. Myriah nodded and started walking across the patio with the dog. "Let's see if any of the people who work in the mall know your owner," she said. "We'll start with the shoe store."

"Want some shoes?" Gabbie asked. "We've got all kinds — yellow, green, and red. And all sizes."

Myriah stopped so suddenly that Chewy stumbled into her. "Not today, thanks," she said very seriously. "I've got a problem. This is a lost dog, and I'm looking for his owner."

"How about some shoes?" Gabbie persisted.

"That's not right," James cried. "You're supposed to talk about the dog, not the shoes."

Myriah frowned. "Think hard," she said to Gabbie. "Have you seen his owner?"

"We have sneakers," Gabbie continued. "And cowboy boots — "

Myriah sighed. Gabbie must have forgotten the script. Myriah would just have to make the best of it. "Let's go, doggie," said Myriah. "Maybe your owner stopped for a slice of pizza." She walked over to the barbecue grill, where Mathew was pretending to throw pizza dough in the air. "Excuse me . . ."

"Not while I'm making the dough," Mathew said. "I can't talk until I get this in the oven."

Myriah looked annoyed. It was obvious that Mathew was adding some new lines to his script. "Look," she said, "this is an emergency."

Mathew shook his head and refused to look at her. He twirled the imaginary dough in his hand, pretending to toss it high in the sky. Finally he spread some pretend-pizza sauce on it and put it in the oven. Then he wiped his hands on a pretend-apron (a nice touch, Jessi thought) and grinned. "Okay, what do you want?"

Myriah repeated the story about the lost dog while Mathew listened intently. "Afraid I can't help you," he said, twirling another piece of dough.

Jessi was beginning to wonder what Myriah would do next when Zach came tearing around the corner on his bicycle. Zach is a good friend of James, but he is very bossy and always tells James what to do.

When he saw Myriah leading Chewy around the patio, he came to a stop. "What are you doing?"

"We're rehearsing a play," Myriah said.

"Can I watch?"

"I guess so," she replied. She waited until Zach settled himself on a huge tire that was suspended from a rope and then went on with the play. She had just taken Chewy into a department store, when Zach burst out laughing.

"This is the dumbest play I've ever seen," he hooted.

"It is not," James said angrily. "I wrote it."

"You *wrote* it?" Zach laughed so hard, he nearly fell off the swing. "It stinks!" He jumped off the tire and headed for his bike. "And what are you doing playing with *girls*, anyway?"

"They're part of the play," James began, his face a bright red.

"I don't believe this," Zachary said, still chuckling. "First you hang around with that retard, Susan Felder, and now you're playing with a bunch of little kids." (Susan Felder is a handicapped girl whose family lives in the neighborhood. She goes to a special school, doesn't talk, and doesn't know how to play with other kids.)

Jessi thought it was really mean of Zach to call her a retard and said so.

"Yeah, well, she is," Zach said bluntly. He wasn't even embarrassed. "You know something, James?" he said, swinging onto his bike. "If you really want to be an American, you've got to change. You need to hang around with me and the other guys. You need to spend more time on your skateboard. And you should dump these girls. Oh, yeah. One more thing. Quit calling your mother 'Mum.' "

James just stood there listening, his hands clenched at his sides. Finally he spoke up. "You know what your problem is, Zach?" he said very quietly. "You're just jealous because you're not in the play."

"He probably can't even act," Mathew said, and Jessi giggled.

"I can so!" Zach said hotly. "Maybe I just don't want to hang around with a bunch of girls!" Zach pedaled as fast as he could down the driveway, chanting, "James is a gi-irl, James is a gi-irl!"

James's face fell, and Jessi felt sorry for him.

Nobody said anything for a moment, and then Chewy barked. "I think he's trying to tell us it's time to go back to the play," James said. Everybody laughed. James clapped his hands loudly. "Okay, places everyone. Let's take it from the top."

Jessi felt very proud of him.

Last Tuesday I got the biggest shock of my life! You're going to really be surprised when I tell you about it.

School had just let out, and Stacey and I had walked Kristy to her bus. Claudia and Mary Anne were trailing behind us, and everyone was trying to decide what to do next.

"Why don't you come over to my house?" Claudia offered. "Mom bought a gallon of Pecan Crunch ice cream." She glanced at Stacey. "And there's homemade applesauce, too. The kind with no sugar."

Stacey smiled. "It sounds good, but I've got an English test tomorrow. So do you, Claudia," she added teasingly. "In case you've forgotten."

Claudia groaned and clutched her head in her hands. "You had to remind me!" She turned to me. "How about you, Dawn?"

I shrugged. I never eat ice cream (I like frozen yogurt and Tofutti) but I didn't want to sound rude. I was just about to make up some excuse not to go to Claudia's when a car horn tooted behind me. I turned automatically and saw — Travis!

"Ohmigosh!" I muttered under my breath.

Mary Anne spotted him at the same time. "Isn't that — "

"Yes, yes," I said quickly, practically fainting on the spot.

"Look, he's pulling over to the curb," Stacey said, grabbing my arm. "And he's waving to you."

My mind went blank. What was Travis doing here? Did he really want to see me?

"Go over to the car," Stacey whispered, giving me a little shove. "What are you waiting for?"

What *was* I waiting for? The best-looking boy I'd ever seen in my whole life was offering me a ride, and I was frozen like a statue! I probably would have stood there forever, except that Stacey jabbed me with her spiral notebook.

"Move!" she ordered.

Travis had already pushed the passenger door open and was flashing his million-dollar smile at me.

"Hop in," he said casually. "Are you on your way home?"

"Yes, but — "

"I've got a better idea," he cut in smoothly. "How'd you like to go shopping with me? I've got to pick out a birthday present for my dad."

I hesitated. Going *anywhere* with Travis would be fantastic, but I knew I should check with Mom first. I shifted from one foot to the other, trying to stall for time. Maybe I could duck back into school and call her first? But then Travis would think that I was a baby! Besides, Mary Anne could always tell Mom and Richard where I was — if she absolutely had to.

Another horn beeped, and Travis patted the front seat of his car. "C'mon," he said urgently. "This is a no-parking zone."

I made up my mind. I dumped my books on the front seat, slid inside, and a minute later we were zipping down the street, with the sounds of hard rock filling the car.

Travis waited till we stopped at a red light to turn to me. "I'm glad you decided to come," he said simply.

I grinned, relaxing a little. "So am I. There's just one thing I should warn you about. I've got to be home by six."

"No problem. We've got plenty of time. I thought we'd hit Surf and Sail first, and then we'll play it by ear." The light changed and he turned left.

"Surf and Sail?" I repeated.

"It's a sporting goods store. My dad has had his eye on a new compass for a long time, and they go on sale this week."

I nodded, happy to be with him. He looked terrific in a blue cotton workshirt and faded jeans. I could hardly *believe* my good luck.

As soon as we stepped into Surf and Sail I knew I was out of my league. I've been sailing plenty of times, but I don't know a whole lot about serious boating equipment. Travis stopped in front of a display case filled with compasses, and I decided to speak up. "Travis, I'm afraid I'm not going to be much help to you. Are you *sure* your father wants a compass?"

Travis laughed and slid his arm around me. "I just wanted an excuse to see you today."

"Really?" I felt a little light-headed. Travis picked out a compass very quickly, and we were back on the sidewalk a few minutes later. Now what? I wondered. I was totally confused. (And a little disappointed. I'd been hoping that Travis would take a long time to make up his mind, so we could spend more time together.)

I started for the car, but he grabbed my elbow and steered me toward Burger Bite. "Aren't we going back home?" I asked.

"We've got hours ahead of us. I thought we'd stop for a snack and then do some more shopping."

I've got to tell you that Burger Bite is not my favorite kind of restaurant, and I was surprised that Travis wanted to go there, too, since he'd said once that he likes health food. Still, I was glad to be sitting in a back booth with him. I reached for a menu, but Travis closed his hand over mine. "We don't need that. I come in here all the time."

But I don't, I longed to say. Travis was obviously planning on ordering for me. I know some girls like it when a boy takes charge like that, but *I* like to make up my own mind. Besides, how could Travis possibly know what I felt like eating?

I practically held my breath when the waitress appeared, and wondered if I should mention that I don't eat meat. I lost my nerve at the last minute, but luckily, Travis ordered grilled cheese sandwiches for both of us.

"So," Travis said when the waitress had left. "What's been happening with you today?"

"Not much, how about you?" I still felt a little tongue-tied around Travis and decided it was easier to let him keep the conversation going. Anyway, he *always* seemed to have something to talk about.

"I tried out for track today," he said earnestly. "You wouldn't believe what happened. I was the first guy the coach picked. I guess all that running I did in California paid off . . ." I let Travis's words drift over me, thinking how wonderful it was to be sitting there with him. If I had to describe the ideal boy, it would be Travis. Tall, good-looking, with a fantastic smile and a great personality. And he liked *me* even though he was three years older than I was.

When the sandwiches arrived a few minutes later, he had moved on to another topic, football. "You see, Coach Larson was demonstrating an intricate play for us," he said, looking into my eyes. He took a bite of sandwich and moved a salt shaker next to the napkin holder. "The quarterback ran down to the twenty-yard line like this . . ." I watched, caught up in the sound of his voice. "And then the tight end zigzagged over here . . ." He picked up a ketchup bottle and plunked it down next to the sugar bowl. "Bingo! Right over the line for a touchdown."

"That's amazing," I said, trying to look impressed.

"And you know what?" he added, sliding the pepper shaker across the table. "I was the only guy there who knew what he was talking about."

"That's wonderful. You really know a lot about football."

Travis grinned. "What can I tell you?" He wolfed down the rest of his sandwich and I hurried to keep up with him.

It was almost four by the time we left Burger Bite, and I was starting to feel a little edgy. I knew Mom wouldn't be thrilled if she found out that I had spent the afternoon with Travis (but I also knew that she and Richard wouldn't be home for another two hours). So I was safe, at least for the moment.

We walked around downtown, and Travis surprised me (as usual) by leading me into the Merry-Go-Round. "I saw some pierced earrings in here that would look great on you," he said. He led me to a display counter and spun an earring tree with his thumb. "Good!

They're still here." He lifted a pair of delicate silver earrings off the tree and held them out to me. "Do you like them?"

They were perfect. Tiny butterflies in flight. "I love them," I said softly.

Travis held them up to my ear and smiled. "I knew they'd be right for you."

"I'll wear them under the stars," I promised him. (I should explain that I wear two earrings in each ear.)

"No," Travis said flatly. "You should wear them up higher. Just get another hole punched in your ear."

"Three holes? I don't know," I said doubtfully. I remembered that I'd had to persuade Mom to let me get my ears pierced in the first place.

Travis laughed. "It's no big deal. All the girls in California wear them that way. It would look really cool on you."

"I'll have to think about it," I said, trying to sound casual.

"There's nothing to it," Travis answered. We were standing side by side at the cashier. "They could probably do it for you right now."

"No!" I was starting to feel a little panicky. I could just imagine Mom's reaction if I did something like that without asking her.

I felt relieved when we left the Merry-Go-Round a few minutes later and headed back to the car, even though I knew that Travis was a tiny bit annoyed with me.

"Thanks for the earrings," I told him, trying to smooth things over.

"I'm glad you like them." He squeezed my arm. I knew I would never, *ever* forget this moment.

My happiness didn't last long though, because when I got home I had the surprise of my life. Mom and Richard were waiting for me in the kitchen.

"You're home early," I said casually, tossing my books on the kitchen table.

"You're home late," Mom answered, frowning a little. She was cutting up vegetables for a salad.

"Um, not really." I nibbled on a carrot, stalling for time. I could tell that Mom and Richard were *both* annoyed with me. What an ending to a perfect day!

"Mary Anne said you went shopping with someone named Travis," Mom went on. "I'd like you to tell me about it." Mom can be *really* direct when she wants to.

There was nothing to do but tell the truth.

"I ran into Travis after school," I said slowly. "He's a friend of mine, and he asked me if I'd like to ride downtown with him — "

"Ride? You went in his car?" Richard interrupted.

"Well, yes. We were going to buy a birthday present for his father," I said quickly.

"Who is this Travis?" Mom said. "And how come he can drive?"

"He's old enough to drive," I told her. "He's sixteen."

Wrong move. Richard looked furious, and Mom looked upset.

"Let me get this straight," Richard said slowly. "You went out with a sixteen-year-old boy in a car? A boy we don't know?"

"Yes, but — "

"But nothing!" Mom said. "You had no business going off like that without asking me first."

I shrugged. This was getting complicated. (And deep down, I had the nagging feeling that Mom was right.)

"Look, why don't we just forget the whole thing and fix dinner? I'll help you," I said, reaching for the salad bowl.

"There's no way we're going to forget this,"

Mom said. She put the knife down and faced me. "No one's going to eat anything until we get this straightened out."

I knew from the look on her face that she meant business. I sat down. I was really in for it.

Mary Anne wandered into the kitchen and stopped dead in her tracks when she saw me. She had "uh-oh" written all over her face. She took her time opening a can of cat food for Tigger, her kitten, and I knew she was listening to every word. If only she hadn't told Mom and Richard that I had been out with Travis!

"We've got a problem here," Richard said flatly. He motioned for me to sit down at the kitchen table.

"I didn't think you would get this upset," I began, but Richard held his hand up.

"You showed very poor judgment, Dawn," he said sternly.

"I know it looks that way, but — "

"I'm very disappointed in you," Mom spoke up. She sat down across from me. I felt like I was being attacked from all sides!

"If you met Travis, you'd really like him,"

I protested. I stared at my hands, not knowing where to begin. "He's really a nice boy."

Mom stared at Richard. "I'm sure he is, but that's not the point."

Mary Anne took a quick peek over her shoulder and went back to feeding Tigger. I couldn't believe all the trouble she had gotten me into.

"Then what's wrong with him?"

"For one thing, he's too old for you," Richard said bluntly. "He's sixteen and you're only thirteen. What could you possibly have in common?"

"Well, we're both from California. We're interested in the same things." I glanced at Mom, wondering if she would agree with me. She should be able to understand how I felt. Even though I love my friends in Connecticut, I miss my friends in California. So does she.

"And another thing," Mom went on, "we've never even met this boy. Did you know he was going to pick you up at school today?"

I shrugged. "Nope. That's just the way Travis is. He likes to do things on the spur of the moment. He's impulsive." *And fun and exciting*, I wanted to add.

"If he really liked you," Richard said, "he

would make plans to see you. He'd visit you here at the house and meet the rest of your family."

I sighed. Richard is very serious about being a good stepfather, but sometimes he just worries too much. I wish he would lighten up a little and be more like Mom.

"Travis likes me," I said. "You wouldn't believe all the presents he's given me. First a necklace and hair combs, and today he bought me some earrings at the Merry-Go-Round."

"I'm not so sure I like that idea," Mom said slowly. "You hardly know him, and he's showering you with presents. Something just isn't right."

I glanced at Mary Anne, who had finished feeding Tigger and was slipping out of the kitchen. I couldn't *wait* to talk to her alone! None of this would have happened if she had kept her mouth shut.

"It's no mystery," I said, scraping my chair back and standing up. "Travis gave me some presents because he likes me. I don't know why you can't understand that." I looked at Mom. "And I *really* want to see him again."

"I know you do, honey," she said, softening a little. "And I'm sure that once we meet him, we'll feel different."

"You mean you're going to let her continue to see him?" Richard exploded. "I can't believe you're serious."

"Well, maybe we came down a little hard on him," Mom said hesitantly. She cupped her chin in her hands and looked thoughtful. "You know, he really does sound nice — "

"This is ridiculous!" Richard broke in. "We don't know this boy at all."

"Now, Richard," Mom said soothingly. "Maybe we're making too big a deal out of this. As long as Dawn understands that she can't see him without our permission, I don't think there's any problem."

"Of course there's a problem. She shouldn't be seeing him at all. He's too old for her."

They were still arguing when I quietly slipped out of the kitchen. It was obvious that the argument was going to go on for a long time, and there was someone I wanted to talk to: Mary Anne. I found her upstairs, sprawled on her bed, doing her homework.

"Thanks a lot," I told her. "You really got me in trouble with Mom and Richard."

"Oh, Dawn, you know I didn't want to do that," she said, sitting up. "I feel awful that they're mad at you, but I didn't know what else to say."

"Why did you have to tell them anything?" I asked, slamming my books on her desk. "You could have kept your mouth shut."

"But how could I have?" Mary Anne said in a quavery voice. "They asked me if I knew where you were. So I had to tell them the truth. I said you had gone shopping. With Travis."

I sighed. I knew Mary Anne couldn't have made up a good lie. Besides, I didn't want her lying for me.

"Anyway, you never said it was a secret." Mary Anne's voice shook a little, and her eyes had grown very bright. "Sharon and Dad would have been really worried about you if I told them I didn't know where you were."

"I know," I said wearily. I had a feeling Mary Anne was about to start crying.

"You know I wouldn't do anything to hurt you," she said, sniffing. Mary Anne cries *very* easily. I didn't say anything for a moment, and then I realized that Mary Anne was right. It wasn't her fault that I was in such a mess.

"Look," I said, putting my arm around her shoulders, "why don't we just forget about it? There's really nothing else you could have done."

She looked up, her eyes teary. "Do you mean that?"

I nodded and sat down on her bed. "How was your day? I've hardly seen you."

"Logan came over after school," she said, brightening a little. "He gave me that toy for Tigger, just like he promised."

Logan is one of the most dependable people I know. He and Mary Anne are a lot alike. You can always count on them, and you always know where you stand with them.

"You really like him, don't you?" I said, even though I knew what her answer would be.

"Of course I do." Mary Anne blushed a little. "I guess that seems silly to you. He's not exciting, like Travis."

"I don't think it's silly. I like Logan."

"He's not full of surprises," Mary Anne said slowly. "But that's okay with me."

I thought about all the problems Travis had caused me today. "Maybe surprises aren't such a great idea after all," I said.

Mom called us for dinner just then, and we didn't have a chance to talk about Logan and Travis anymore. I slid into my place at the dining room table and had no idea what to expect. Would Mom and Richard argue all during dinner? Would I get a lecture? Would they criticize Travis?

Luckily, none of these things happened, and dinner went fairly smoothly, considering the circumstances. But Mom and Richard didn't say much during the meal. Mom just stared at a spot over my head, and Richard pretended to be absorbed in his Greek salad. Mary Anne and I exchanged a look now and then, but neither one of us felt much like talking. However, I had the feeling that this wasn't the last I would hear about Travis.

Saturday

Today I baby-sat for my younger brothers and sisters and they had a terrific time outdoors playing one of Karen's favorite games -- "Going Camping." It's easy because it's mostly make-believe. All we used today were an old bedspread, some chairs, a few props, and lots of imagination. Karen supplied plenty of that! The best part is that big kids and little kids can play, and it can go on for hours. I guess the only other thing you need is a sunny day, but come to think of it, you could probably move the tent into the living room!

Kristy always likes to give a lot of details about her baby-sitting jobs because she expects the club members to read the notebook very carefully. It's a great way to learn what other baby-sitters are doing with their kids, and you can get a lot of good ideas. None of us really likes to write in the notebook, but Kristy takes her job as president very seriously, and she tries to set an example for us.

"Going Camping" was the perfect way to entertain her four younger brothers and sisters. Karen has a great imagination and loves *any* kind of game that involves "let's pretend." David Michael is an easygoing kid who will go along with just about any game you suggest. And Andrew and Emily love to play, period!

This is the way Kristy and Karen set up the game. They found an old bedspread upstairs in the linen closet. It had belonged to Andrew and was bright yellow with racing cars all over it.

"It doesn't look like a real tent," David Michael said doubtfully when Kristy and Karen brought it downstairs. "It should be dark green, or maybe brown."

"No, this is fine," Kristy said hastily. She

knew the kids were getting restless, and she wanted to start things moving as quickly as possible.

"I'll help!" Karen yelled when Kristy started to drape the bedspread over some lawn chairs.

"Make it a *big* tent," David Michael suggested. "Then we can move all our supplies inside." He picked up a brown canvas canteen and a cast-iron frying pan.

"Big ant?" Emily said, puzzled. Emily is learning English sort of slowly. The pediatrician says she's language-delayed.

Andrew laughed. "No, big *tent*," he said, pointing to the bedspread. "C'mon inside."

"Wait! Don't go in yet!" Karen said urgently.

Kristy looked startled. "Why not?"

Karen lowered her voice to a whisper. "Because you can't just walk into a tent without looking. You have to check it first for bears. There could be one sleeping inside."

"Bears?" Emily started to look a little worried.

"It's just pretend," Kristy said, taking her hand. Karen is *very* imaginative, and when you set up a pretend situation, she jumps right in. "What should we do?" Kristy asked very seriously. She was still holding onto Emily's hand. She didn't want to squelch Karen's imagination, but she didn't want Emily to be frightened, either.

Karen thought for a moment. "I'll go in first," she said. She picked up a broken flashlight. "If I'm not back in a few minutes, you better call the mountain rangers."

"Good idea," David Michael told her. "I think I can signal them. It's a good thing I know Morse code." He scrambled through a cigar box filled with toys and picked out a set of fake teeth. He clicked the teeth together a few times. "We're lucky this is still working."

"I want to do Morse code! I want to do Morse code!" Andrew shouted.

"Sssh," Karen said. "You'll wake up the bear if he's sleeping inside. Do you know how mad they get if you wake them up when they're hibernating? That's all we need!"

"Sorry," Andrew said, clapping his hand over his mouth. "Please can I do Morse code?" he whispered.

David Michael handed him the plastic teeth. "Just remember that SOS is three short, three long, and three short. You got it?" He clicked the teeth together to show him.

"I got it."

"Places everyone," Karen said. "I'm going in now. Andrew, are you ready?"

"I'm ready with the teeth. I mean the Morse code!"

"David Michael?"

"I'm standing by with the — " He spotted a pile of branches nearby. "The bonfire!"

"Why do we need a bonfire?" Kristy asked.

David Michael rolled his eyes. "In case the Morse code doesn't work. I can always light the bonfire and use smoke signals to get the mountain ranger."

"Oh, right. Good idea." Kristy smiled to herself. The kids were *really* getting into it. She could hardly wait to tell the BSC members this at the next club meeting.

"Me, too! Me, too! Me, too!" Emily said, tugging at Karen's T-shirt.

"She wants something to do," Kristy said. "Let's give her a job."

"I know. You can wish me luck. I have a very dangerous job ahead of me," Karen said seriously. She walked over to Emily and shook hands. "Say 'Good luck,' " she prompted.

"Good luck," Emily said, smiling. Kristy had no idea if she knew what 'good luck' meant, but she knew Emily was happy to be included.

"Here goes," Karen said dramatically. She took a deep breath and crawled inside the tent.

Everyone else crouched down and waited outside, ready to run, if necessary. A few moments passed, and then Karen reappeared. "It's all safe," she said. "There are no bears inside. At least right this minute."

"What do you mean, right this minute?" David Michael asked.

Karen looked over her shoulder as if she expected a bear to appear at any moment. "I don't want to scare anyone," she said slowly, "but I have to warn you that I found a pot of honey inside."

"Honey!" Andrew clapped his hands over his mouth.

Karen nodded. "And you know what that means," she said, looking around the group.

"What does it mean?" David Michael looked blank.

Karen nudged him. "It means there must have been a *bear* in there."

"Oh, right." David Michael scuffed the dirt with his toe and looked a little embarrassed. "So what do we do now?"

"Well, I think we should all go into the tent," Karen said, holding the flap open. "But make sure you rig up a bear alert outside for us."

"A bear alert?" David Michael brightened.

"That's a great idea. You go in and I'll fix one."

Kristy trooped inside with the younger kids, and for a minute everyone was quiet. It was pretty hot and uncomfortable in the tent, and she wondered what Karen was going to come up with next. Luckily she didn't have to wait long.

Emily was yawning when Karen grabbed Kristy's arm. "Did you feel that?"

"Feel what?" Kristy asked.

"The ground just shook," Karen said, looking at each of the kids. "I think we're in for an earthquake."

"No!" Andrew screamed. "What should we do?"

"Let's all hold hands," Karen said calmly. "That way nobody will be swept away when it happens again."

Emily glanced at Kristy, her eyes wide as saucers, and Kristy scooped her onto her lap. "Don't worry, Emily," she said, holding her very tightly. "I'm not going to let anything happen to you."

"There it goes again," Karen said. She fell against the side of the tent, and Andrew did the same thing. "Hold on tight, everybody!"

"Wait a minute," Andrew yelled. "What

about David Michael? He's outside making that dumb bear alert!"

"We'll have to help him," Karen said firmly. "Andrew, rescue David Michael."

Andrew looked impressed. "Wow!"

"Open the flap of the tent *very* carefully and peek outside. The minute you see him, tell him to get in here."

"Okay." Andrew crawled to the edge of the tent and lifted the bedspread. "David Michael! David Michael!" he whispered. "Come inside. I've got to rescue you." He crawled back inside. "He's not there!"

"Are you sure?" Karen asked.

"I'm sure!"

Karen sighed. "This is much worse than I thought."

"Do you think the earthquake got him?" Andrew asked.

"No, I think . . . Morbidda Destiny got him!"

Kristy tried not to laugh. Morbidda Destiny is the old lady who lives next door. Her real name is Mrs. Porter, but Karen is convinced that she's a witch. She lives in an old Victorian house with gables and turrets, and she even keeps a broomstick on the front porch.

"Now what will we do?" asked Andrew.

Karen looked stumped. "I don't know. Morbidda Destiny has special powers. She could turn David Michael into a witch if she wanted to, or she might make him drink a magic potion."

"No!"

Karen nodded. "She might even make boystew out of him."

"Ew, gross," Andrew muttered. "How can we save him?"

"Let me think," Karen said, just as the tent flap opened and David Michael crawled in.

"The bear alert is in place," he said, scooting over to Kristy. "You'll all be safe."

"Are you okay?" Karen asked him. "We thought Morbidda Destiny got you."

David Michael laughed. "Of course I'm okay."

Karen looked at him suspiciously, as if he really might be a newt or a toad pretending to be David Michael. "I guess so. Where were you when Andrew called you?"

"I was hiding," he said teasingly. "I knew you'd figure that Morbidda Destiny had kidnapped me, and I wanted to see what you'd do about it."

"Well, it wasn't funny," Karen said sternly. Andrew started telling David Michael about the earthquake, and Karen sat down next to Kristy. "You know what I think?" she whispered in Kristy's ear. "I think Morbidda Destiny really *did* get him and made him *say* that he was hiding!"

"Do you really think so?" asked Kristy.

Karen nodded. "Witches have their ways," she said mysteriously.

"You've got to give Chewy a doggie treat or he's going to ruin the play!" Myriah cried.

It was a Thursday afternoon, and I was baby-sitting for the three younger Hobart kids while Ben was at a dentist appointment. Mathew, James, and Johnny were in the backyard rehearsing their play with Myriah and Gabbie Perkins.

"We can give him a yum-yum if you want," I suggested, "but I don't think it will help." Chewbacca, the hero of the play, was tearing around and around the yard. I've never seen a dog with less acting ability. He was supposed to act sad and lonely (according to the script James wrote), but he was running in circles, yapping and wagging his tail. Every once in a while he'd snap at an imaginary fly.

"Come here, Chewy," I said wearily. "Let's see if this calms you down." I popped a doggie treat into his mouth. He immediately sat up on his hind legs and begged for more.

"I told you it wouldn't help," James said. "That dog can't act."

"He can so!" Myriah put her arms around Chewy's furry neck. "He just doesn't feel like it."

"Let's take it from the top. Start the mall scene again," James ordered. "Does everybody remember what they're supposed to do?" He glanced at his notes. "Gabbie, you own a shoe store."

"Shoes, shoes," she sang. I put my fingers to my lips to remind her to be quiet, and she grinned at me.

"Mathew, you work in the pizza place, and Johnny, you work in a pet store."

"I want to work in a pet store!" said Gabbie. "Pets for sale! Pets for sale! We have rabbits, gerbils, and hamsters. Maybe even cats and dogs — "

"No, Gabbie," James said quietly. "You stay in your shoe store and sell shoes. You have a very important part in the play." Gabbie beamed. That was the best thing that James could have said to her.

"Now can we *please* begin?" James said.

"Shoe sale! Shoe sale!" Gabbie chanted.

"Come buy some shoes. We have specials today."

"Myriah, you can make your entrance now," James said. "Quiet, everybody." He sat down next to me at the picnic table. Nobody moved. "Myriah, what are you waiting for?" he yelled.

She stared at him, her hand on Chewy's neck. "We're waiting for you to cue us," she said. "That's the way they do it in the movies. You're supposed to say, 'And . . . action!' "

James rolled his eyes. "All right, all right," he muttered. "And . . . action!"

I smiled.

The scene started smoothly. Myriah was talking softly to Chewy, asking if he was lost, when suddenly earsplitting rock music filled the air.

"Who turned on that radio?" James demanded. He jumped up and raced over to Mathew, who was sitting in a red wagon. "Mathew, what do you think you're doing?" He reached into the wagon and pulled out a small radio. "You're ruining the scene. We can't hear Myriah's lines."

Mathew shrugged. "I'm playing music in my pizza parlor."

Myriah frowned. "Mathew, you can't make

noise when someone else is saying their lines. That's the first thing you have to learn when you put on a play."

"But I don't have anything to do. Nobody gave me any lines."

"You have lines in the next scene," James told him. "Look, all you have to do right now is stay in your place and act like you're making pizzas."

"I know what I could do," Mathew said. "If you give me my radio back, I could listen to music through my headphones."

James hesitated. "I guess that would be okay. Just make sure you pay attention so you don't miss your cue. Myriah is going to visit all the stores in the mall, and you're the second place she goes."

Myriah shifted impatiently. "Can we start over now? Chewy's getting restless."

"Okay," James said. I could tell he was getting a little annoyed at all the interruptions. "Places everyone."

"You're at it again? I don't believe it!" exclaimed a voice.

I turned to see Zach steer his bike toward the picnic table, where James and I were sitting. "I thought you had enough of this baby stuff the other day."

"It's not baby stuff," Myriah said, insulted. "We're putting on a *real* play."

"Yeah, yeah." Zach plopped himself down next to James and punched him playfully in the arm. "So what do you say we play some football?"

"He can't leave rehearsal," Myriah said. "We're right in the middle of a very important scene."

"I bet!" Zach snorted. "What kind of a play has a *dog* in it? You must be doing *Annie*."

"No. I already told you. It's a play I wrote myself," James said shyly. Zach doubled up with laughter and nearly fell off the picnic bench.

"I know, I know." He socked James again, this time on the shoulder. "When are you going to grow up and do some guy stuff?"

"Guy stuff?"

Zach leaned close to him. "You know, football, skateboarding, things like that."

"I do a lot of sports," James said stiffly. I could tell he was embarrassed because two little pinpoints of color had appeared on his cheeks.

"You could have fooled me!" Zach hooted. "Every time I see you, you're hanging around with a bunch of girls." He paused. "You know, you're never going to be popular at this rate. The kids at school still think you're weird."

"Weird?"

Zach nodded. "Can you blame them? You don't talk right, you don't go out with the guys, and worst of all, you hang around with girls."

James hung his head and looked sheepish. "I don't want anybody to think I'm weird."

"Well, of course you don't," Zach said, slapping him on the back. "But you can change all that. Just start doing things differently. And you can start right now."

"I can?"

"Sure." Zach stood up and got on his bike. "Come on back to my house and we'll toss a football around. Then we'll watch a new horror movie I just rented. Oh, yeah, and we'll work on talking like a real American." He released the kickstand on his bike, ready to go. "Sound good?"

James hesitated, and then tossed his script on the picnic table. "You're on!" he said.

"James," Myriah wailed. "What about the play?"

James shook his head and didn't answer. He was already on the way to the garage for his bike.

"Now what will we do?" Mathew asked. "We can't put on the play without James."

"We'll think of something else to do," I promised him. I watched as Zach and James pedaled down the driveway. Why did James let Zach talk to him that way? And why did he want to change his whole personality to please Zach? James was a great kid, just the way he was. Zach had no business telling him how to talk or how to act. Why did James let him get away with it? None of it made any sense to me, and I was *very* disappointed in James.

Kristy dropped a bomb and didn't even know it. It all started at our Monday afternoon BSC meeting in Claudia's room. Jessi mentioned Jackie Rodowsky, the "walking disaster," and everyone started telling funny stories about him. In case you don't know, Jackie is a really cute seven-year-old with flaming red hair and freckles. He is also accident-prone.

"Do you remember the day I took Jackie to the pool?" Kristy said. "First he got stung by a bee, and then he got lost and almost gave me a heart attack. My brother Sam told one of the girls in his class about it, and she said she saw the whole thing. She was working as a lifeguard that day."

"Really? Who was it?" Mary Anne asked.

"I don't know her name, but she's this *fantastic*-looking girl who's captain of the swim team at Stoneybrook High School." Kristy picked up her clipboard, ready to get back to business. "Sam says she's the reason Travis tried out for swimming along with all his other sports. I hear he's really crazy about her. They've been dating for weeks."

I looked up from the club notebook in total shock. Travis was *dating* someone? Travis was *crazy* about someone? How could that be possible? He was interested in *me!* I could feel my cheeks burning, and I wondered if anyone else noticed. I started thumbing through a *Seventeen* magazine, hoping Kristy wouldn't get annoyed with me.

The club meeting went on as usual and a few minutes later, I actually managed to take a phone call from Dr. Johanssen, who needed a sitter for Charlotte. My voice sounded a little shaky, but I wrote down all the details about the job and promised to call her back.

"Now, who gets the job?" Kristy asked brightly, as Mary Anne checked the record book.

I returned to the *Seventeen* magazine, dying for the meeting to be over. What was going on with Travis? Could Kristy be mistaken? I couldn't wait to get home and figure everything out.

Unfortunately, Mom asked me to make a

salad the minute I walked in the door. It was the last thing in the world I felt like doing, but what could I say? Mary Anne made spaghetti, Mom made the sauce (meatless), Richard made garlic bread, and before I knew it, all four of us were eating dinner together.

I was there, but I wasn't there. Does that make sense? I was sitting at the dining room table, passing the salad and half listening to Mary Anne talk about school, but my mind was a million miles away. I could have been on another planet! My brain was churning, trying to come up with an explanation for what Kristy had said about Travis.

I hated to admit it, but there just weren't that many possibilities. I didn't really think that Kristy had made a mistake, because she had seemed so definite about it. She had mentioned Travis by name (and how many Travises could there be at SHS?).

Then I let my mind play a little game. Maybe there was a really farfetched reason for Travis's behavior. Maybe he was just pretending to like this girl. But why? I was stumped. Unless . . . maybe Travis *wanted* to join the swim team, too, and he figured one way to do it would be to date the captain. But wait a minute. Travis was a great athlete (he said so himself), so why would he need extra pull? Nothing made sense. There *was* no explanation for the way Travis was acting.

I said so later that evening to Mary Anne, when we were upstairs working hard in my room. (Sometimes we do our homework together.) That night, Mary Anne was solving math problems, and I was trying to figure out Travis.

"You know, it just doesn't make sense," I blurted out.

"What doesn't?" Mary Anne barely looked up from her book.

"What Kristy said about Travis and that lifeguard!" My voice was so loud it startled her.

"Oh, that." She pushed her papers aside and stared at me.

"Well, what did you think about it?" I said impatiently.

Mary Anne shrugged. "I guess I didn't think much about it either way. Did it bother you?"

Did it bother me! "Yes," I said with clenched teeth. "It bothered me a lot."

Mary Anne sighed. "Then I wish she hadn't brought it up."

"No, I'm glad she did. Maybe this way I can figure out what's going on. I don't know why he's taking out someone else. And I'm not sure why he's paying attention to me." I started pacing restlessly back and forth in front of the dresser.

"Dawn, it's not the end of the world. I wish you weren't so unhappy about it." Sometimes Mary Anne gets really upset over other people's problems, but she's usually a good person to talk to.

"But I thought Travis cared about *me!*"

Mary Anne hesitated. "I'm sure he does. But he can take out anyone he wants to. It's not like the two of you are going steady. Anyway, she's probably a lot closer to him in age."

"But why is he paying so much attention to me? I thought he really liked me."

"I guess he likes her, too. There's nothing wrong with that, is there?"

I was all set to argue, and then I stopped myself. What Mary Anne was saying made sense, even though it killed me to admit it. Travis and I didn't have a formal relationship the way Mary Anne and Logan have. In a way, I envy Mary Anne, because she always knows where she stands with Logan. And he knows where he stands with her. But Travis is the type of boy who keeps you guessing. He's full of surprises (the lifeguard was a big one!), and I'd have to figure out a way to handle it.

Later that night, as I turned out my light, the idea came to me in a flash. The best way to find out how Travis felt about this girl was to see the two of them together. And that was exactly what I was going to do.

I got my chance a few days later. It was a sunny Thursday afternoon, and my teacher decided to let our class out ten minutes early. I raced across the school yard, a plan already forming in my mind. If I hurried, I could just get to SHS before the dismissal bell rang.

The SHS kids were barreling down the broad stone steps of the school as I came tearing around the corner. My heart sank. How would I ever find Travis in this huge mob? I was just trying to decide where to stand to get the best view, when I had an incredible stroke of luck. I spotted Travis pausing in the doorway to put on his sunglasses. He looked terrific in faded jeans and a white T-shirt, and my heart did a little flip-flop. I was dying to run up to him and tell him how glad I was to see him.

But he wasn't alone. He turned around and linked arms with a great-looking girl. Her long red hair tumbled down her back, and she had high cheekbones, just like a model. She was dressed in a white cotton flight suit, exactly the kind of trendy outfit that Claudia or Stacey would wear. I hated her on sight, and then I stopped and reminded myself that it wasn't her fault she was gorgeous. And it wasn't her fault that Travis liked her.

Travis and the girl headed for the sidewalk, and I held my breath, hoping that Travis didn't have his car. Another stroke of luck. They walked right past the school parking lot, still arm in arm. They were probably going downtown (another shopping trip?) and if I was very careful, I'd be able to follow them. I waited behind a tree until they were a good half block ahead of me.

I had to know what Travis was up to.

A few minutes later, I decided I wasn't cut out to be a spy. Do you know how hard it is to follow someone? (I know what you're probably thinking. How can I say that when it looks so easy on television?)

But I had two disasters almost immediately. First, I stepped into a huge puddle, ruining my new shoes, and then I was nearly run over by a garbage truck. I was so busy watching Travis that I didn't even notice the light had changed, and I stepped right out into the intersection. Dumb!

I took a deep breath and told myself to calm down. I would never find out the truth about Travis if I were flattened by a truck. The trick was to stay cool.

I made sure Travis and the girl stayed at least half a block ahead of me. With any luck, I'd be able to blend into the crowd once we got downtown. The tricky part was a long stretch of a street with a narrow sidewalk and very few trees. I knew that if Travis turned around for any reason, he would spot me.

I was being extra cautious when a car horn blasted right behind me. I nearly jumped out of my skin! To my horror, Travis heard it, too. He glanced over his shoulder, and I barely had time to dart behind a bush. Had he seen me? I had no idea, but I wasn't taking any chances. I crouched behind the bush, feeling a little silly, but afraid to get up. I counted silently to ten and then took up the chase once more.

A few minutes later we reached downtown Stoneybrook. Travis and the girl stopped first at Burger Bite, and I watched them head for a back booth. Would he order for her? I wondered. I took a seat near the front door and peeked out from underneath a giant menu. If I scrunched around in my seat, I could see the two of them in the mirror.

They were laughing and talking, and when the girl picked up the menu, Travis closed his hand over hers. He winked at her before he gave their order to the waitress. My heart sank. The smiles, the tender looks . . . it was all so familiar. Travis was staring at her as if she were the only girl in the room. He had looked at me in exactly the same way!

I gulped down a lemonade and quietly left the restaurant. My heart was pounding in my chest as I sat on a bench across the street from the Burger Bite. I decided to wait for them to come out and then follow them to their next stop. Why was I doing this? I can't even explain it. I just *had* to know what they were going to do next, even though I knew it was going to hurt me.

About half an hour later, they came out arm in arm and headed for the Merry-Go-Round. Hamburgers and pierced earrings. Sounds familiar, doesn't it? Travis was taking her to *exactly* the same places he had taken me. I wondered for one crazy moment if Travis would even buy her the same earrings he had bought for me. (Not that it would matter at this point.)

They didn't buy anything, but they wandered up and down the aisles, looking at the jewelry. They kept their heads close together, laughing and talking. Even though I couldn't hear what they were saying, I could see that they were having a terrific time together. Why couldn't I have been the one with Travis? My chest felt so tight, I thought it would explode, but I forced myself to keep watching them. I should have known that things could only get worse.

It was late afternoon when they finally finished their window shopping and headed away from town. I tagged along after them, feeling tired and discouraged. (And very jealous.) There were so many thoughts crowding in my head at once that it was impossible to think clearly. Why was Travis so interested in this girl? Yes, I know she was great-looking, but it had to be more than that. Travis had told me over and over how beautiful my eyes were, and he had even picked out combs for me to wear in my hair. So that must mean that he thought I was pretty good-looking, didn't it? What did she have that I didn't have?

I was trying to sort everything out when Travis and the girl suddenly entered a small park. I barely had time to duck into a bus shelter when the two of them sat down on a bench just a few feet away. Now what?

I didn't have to wait long. I watched in horror as Travis leaned over and *kissed* her! I know I gasped out loud, but both of them were too busy to notice. My hand flew up to my mouth, and I felt hot tears stinging my eyelids. How could this be happening?

I don't know how long they would have

stayed in the park, but suddenly a group of little kids sat down next to them. I saw Travis frown and then laughingly pull the redhead to her feet. She laid her head against his shoulder, just for a moment, and then the two of them moved off again, arm in arm. I felt like staying right in the bus shelter and crying my eyes out, but I knew I had to keep going.

Half a block later, they stopped at the movie theater and looked at the marquee. The way they were nodding and talking, it was obvious that they were making plans to go to a movie together. That night? That weekend? I had no way of knowing, but it didn't really matter. All that mattered was that *she* would be with Travis, and I wouldn't. Their fingers were laced tightly together, and I saw the look in Travis's eyes when he smiled at her. He should be smiling that way at *me*.

I had seen enough. It was nearly dusk, and I hurried home, thinking, thinking, thinking. Did Travis like this girl because she was his own age? Was I really "too young" for him, just like Richard had said? Was Travis annoyed with me because I hadn't taken his advice and had that third hole pierced in my ear? Surely he wouldn't get so mad over a little thing like that? No matter how hard I tried to explain things, my mind kept coming back to one point: Travis didn't care about me at all. How could I have been so mistaken about him?

I was still *very* upset over Travis when we had our next BSC meeting. I had made up my mind not to say anything to my friends, but somehow everything came pouring out.

We were waiting around for phone calls when Kristy mentioned that Sam and Travis were on the track team together. "I don't know how Travis does it," Kristy said admiringly. "He's playing three different sports this season, and he's even talking about trying out for the school play."

"He should," Stacey piped up. "Can you imagine how great he'd look onstage? He's gorgeous! He has the dreamiest eyes I've ever seen."

Stacey (who happens to be a little boy-crazy) was all set to launch into a long description of Travis's smile, when I cut her off.

"Please, can we change the subject?" I pleaded. I jumped up and grabbed my jacket. "If we're just going to sit around and talk about boys, I'm going home. I've got better things to do."

Kristy looked shocked, and Stacey gave me a long look. "Dawn, what's wrong?" she asked.

"Nothing," I snapped. I turned around so my friends couldn't see the tears that were threatening to spill down my cheeks. "I've just heard enough about Travis, that's all. In fact, I've heard *more* than enough!" I stumbled blindly toward the door to Claudia's room, but Mary Anne stopped me.

"Wait, Dawn," she said softly. "You might as well tell everyone what's going on."

"I don't want to get into it," I said stiffly.

Mary Anne took my hand and pulled me gently onto Claud's bed. "That's what friends are for, you know. We're all here for each other."

I hesitated. Everyone was looking at me, and they all seemed worried. Maybe it was better to get things out into the open.

"I saw Travis with someone else," I said slowly. "Probably the captain of the swim team. That's why I'm so upset."

Stacey looked puzzled. "Why would that bother you? Unless — " She clapped her hand over her mouth. "Are you going out with him? Oh, wow! When did all this happen?"

I shrugged. "We're not really going out together, but I know he cares about me. I mean, I *thought* he cared about me." I told them about the surprise visit at the house, and the necklace and hair combs. (Also the trip to Burger Bite and the Merry-Go-Round.) I left out the part about Mom and Richard being so angry with me.

"That rat," Stacey said angrily after I told them about Travis kissing the girl in the park. "Why did he lead you on like that?"

"He didn't really lead her on," Kristy said. "Don't forget, he never really asked her out. At least, not on a real date."

"Oh, Kristy," Claudia said. "You're being much too practical. If somebody visits you at your house and brings you presents, it's like a date. And if they take you shopping after school, that's like a date, too."

"It is?" Jessi asked. She and Mallory had been following the whole conversation without saying a word.

Claudia unwrapped a Hershey's Kiss and popped it into her mouth. "Well, sort of. At least I think it is."

"I think so, too," Stacey said. "Travis gave Dawn the idea that he liked her, so he's definitely a creep."

I sighed. I was glad that my friends were

all taking my side, but I didn't feel much better. My chest ached every time I thought about Travis.

"Don't worry, Dawn," Claudia said. "You'll meet someone a million times nicer than Travis. Someone who *appreciates* you."

I sniffled a little. How could there be anybody nicer than Travis?

"In fact," Mary Anne said, "I think I know just the person."

"You do?" Kristy asked. "Tell us about him."

Mary Anne grinned. "Well, he's fourteen, and he's fantastic-looking. Plus he's got a great sense of humor, and he's supposed to be *really* nice."

"Supposed to be?" Kristy raised her eyebrows. "Don't you know for sure?"

"I'm sure," Mary Anne said. "It's just that I haven't met him yet."

"Who is he?" Jessi asked. "Does he go to SMS?"

"No, he's from out of town." She paused. "He's Logan's cousin. His name is Lewis and he's coming here for a visit soon." She bent down so we were on eye level. "And guess what? He doesn't have a girlfriend."

Mary Anne looked quite pleased with herself. I didn't want to sound ungrateful, but I had no desire to meet Lewis. I didn't care how nice he was or how handsome or funny. I wanted Travis. Why couldn't everyone understand that?

"Isn't it wonderful?" Mary Anne went on, all smiles.

I blew my nose and tried to look interested. There was no point in hurting Mary Anne's feelings, and I could always make up some excuse for not seeing Lewis when he got here.

"Wonderful," I said. "Just wonderful."

CHAPTER 12

Tuesday

When I sat for the Hobarts today, I walked into the middle of James's play. I was just settling down for a game of Chinese checkers when James announced that it was "show time." He insisted that I see Little Dog Lost (the play he had written). Several of you other BSC members have already seen it, and he wanted me to see it, too. Plus he had an actual audience this time. The play was a big hit!

"Please, Mary Anne," Mathew and Myriah chanted together. "We want to do the play for a big audience today. It's really ready."

"I thought we'd play checkers," Mary Anne said, "and then we'd make brownies together."

"Brownies! We can have brownies *anytime*," said Myriah. "This is important stuff. This is a play!"

"Please!" Gabbie squealed. "No brownies! No checkers! Don't you want everyone to see *Little Dog Lost*?"

"Well, sure," Mary Anne replied. "Of course I do." Mary Anne knew the play from reading Kristy's and Jessi's baby-sitting notes. They had seen the play "in rehearsal" and Mary Anne guessed that the kids had been working on it a lot since then.

She glanced at James, who was looking very pleased with himself. "Are you ready to do this?"

He nodded. "As ready as we'll ever be. Everybody knows their lines, and if Chewy stays under control, we'll be fine."

Chewy! Mary Anne's heart sank. She had forgotten that Chewy was the star of the play. "Where is Chewy?" Mary Anne asked.

"He's all ready!" Gabbie informed her. "He's waiting in the garage." She looked at James. "We call that offstage."

"I see." Mary Anne watched as Gabbie opened the garage door and Chewy came barreling across the yard. He acted like a dog who had been cooped up for five years. He immediately began running in circles.

"He's excited," Myriah explained.

"I can see that." Mary Anne gently pushed Chewy off the lawn chair he'd jumped on. "Are you sure he'll calm down enough for the play?"

"I know he will," Myriah said, petting him. "I'll put him back in the garage."

Mary Anne doubted that Chewy would calm down, but she didn't want to discourage Myriah. "Okay," she said finally, "where do we start?"

"We need to set up chairs for the audience, and then we need to start ringing doorbells." James was suddenly very businesslike as he dragged some folding chairs over to the patio. "This is the stage," he said, motioning to the backyard, "and this is where the audience sits."

"That looks fine, but what did you mean about ringing doorbells?"

"To tell people about the play," said Mathew impatiently.

"We really should have sent out invitations," Myriah said, "but we've been so busy rehearsing, we didn't get around to it." She looked a little worried. "It's not too late to ask people to come, is it?"

"I guess not." Mary Anne glanced at her watch. It was after three-thirty. "But we better get started right away. How about if I call Mallory Pike and see if she can bring some of her brothers and sisters?"

"Oh, good!" Myriah clapped her hands together. "And ask Jessi to bring Becca and Squirt."

"The more the better," James said. "The grown-ups can sit on the folding chairs, and the little kids can sit on blankets."

"Are we inviting grown-ups?" asked Mary Anne.

"Of course! Otherwise it won't seem like a real play," James replied.

"Hmm, I guess you're right." Where could Mary Anne find some real live parents at a moment's notice? she wondered. She thought of Mrs. Pike. As far as she knew, Mal's mom was the only one of our clients who might be at home.

A quick phone call to Mrs. Pike settled things.

"Of course I'll come, Mary Anne," she said warmly. "Stacey took a couple of kids to the playground, but I'll round them up along with Vanessa and the triplets. I know they'd love to see a play."

Half an hour later, everything was falling into place. Mal (who was baby-sitting for Charlotte Johanssen) arrived with Charlotte and her best friend, Becca Ramsey. Jessi brought the Newton kids. Stacey arrived a few minutes later with two of the Pike kids — Margo, who is seven, and Claire, who is five.

"Hi, Mary Anne-silly-billy-goo-goo!" Claire shouted. (Claire is going through an extremely silly stage right now.)

Mary Anne was helping everyone find seats when Claudia appeared. "I just heard about the play," Claud whispered. "I'll help seat people if you want to go help James. He looks like he's got a problem."

Mary Anne glanced up. James was darting back and forth with a clipboard, barking orders to his actors. "Johnny, I want you to be quiet until it's time for you to say your lines!"

"*Little dog lost,*" he sang softly.

James put his finger to his lips. "No talking," he said sternly.

"I wasn't talking. I was singing," Johnny said, making a face.

James looked like he wanted to throw his clipboard in the air. Mary Anne touched his shoulder. "I'll make sure the younger kids are in their places," she told him. "Why don't you do something about Chewy? He's making a racket in the garage, and I'm afraid someone's going to let him out."

"Let him out?" Myriah repeated. "*Oh*, no!" She grabbed a Magic Marker and a piece of paper and told Mary Anne to make a sign that read: STAR'S DRESSING ROOM. KEEP OUT!

Mary Anne smiled. "I think that'll do it," she said.

The audience was settling down and James edged over to Mary Anne.

"Do you think I should say something to the audience?" He looked a little nervous.

Mary Anne nodded. "You'll have to introduce the play. After all, they don't even have programs."

"I feel a little silly."

"Don't feel silly. And remember to tell everyone that you *wrote* the play."

"Do you think so?"

"Of course. You should be very proud. Not many kids your age could write a play."

James smiled then, and Mary Anne knew he was relaxing a little. A few minutes later, he cleared his throat and stepped in front of the crowd. Mary Anne crossed her fingers as he finished the introduction and took a seat in the front row. It was show time!

Myriah made her entrance like a professional actress. She was wearing one of Mrs. Perkins's coats and was carrying a large pocketbook.

"Oh, I just love shopping at the mall," she said brightly.

"Hi, Myriah-silly-billy-goo-goo!" Claire shouted from the audience.

Myriah frowned but stayed in character. "Where shall I go first?" she said, coming close to the audience. "There are so many stores to choose from."

Mary Anne knew that Chewy was supposed to be onstage by that point, but there was no sign of him. James turned around from the front row and caught her eye. "Get Chewy fast!" he mouthed.

Mary Anne grabbed Johnny Hobart, who didn't have to go onstage for awhile. "Quick,

Johnny," Mary Anne hissed. "Let Chewy out of the garage!"

Johnny stared at her. "I already did," he said solemnly.

"Then where is he?"

Johnny pointed toward the Perkinses' yard, where Chewy was digging an enormous hole in the flower garden.

"Oh, no!" Mary Anne wailed.

"I can whistle for him," Johnny suggested.

"Do it!"

Johnny stuck two fingers in his mouth and made an earsplitting sound. Chewy bounded across the lawn, knocked over Gabbie's "shoe store," and skidded to a stop at Johnny's feet.

The kids in the audience started laughing, not sure if this was supposed to be part of the show. Mary Anne knew she had to act fast. She grabbed Chewy's collar and pushed him "onstage."

"Go on. Act like you're lost," she pleaded.

Myriah waited until Chewy raced over to her, and then she sank down to her knees. "Oh, you poor dog," she cried. "You're lost and looking for your owner." Chewy immediately began licking her face, nearly beside himself with joy. "You must be very . . . sad," she said doubtfully.

Someone in the audience giggled at this line, because Chewy was running in circles and barking. He didn't look the least bit sad!

Myriah decided to ad-lib some lines. "Sometimes dogs *act* happy, but they're really sad. And *lost*," she added, in case the little kids in the audience had missed the point.

James signaled to Myriah to begin her walk through the "mall," and she headed for Gabbie, who was rearranging her shoe store.

"Shoe sale! Shoe sale!" Gabbie yelled, picking up a decrepit shoe. It was muddy from Chewy's mad dash through the yard. Everybody laughed at her line, and Gabbie looked pleased.

James rolled his eyes. Mary Anne knew the play wasn't turning out at all as he expected, but at least he was getting a lot of laughs. And then *Mary Anne* got a surprise. She was standing at the back of the patio when Zach showed up! He was the last person in the world she wanted to see at the play.

Mary Anne wasn't taking any chances. She showed him to a seat way in the back of the audience, and decided to sit next to him. "It's a great play," she whispered. "Really funny."

"Uh-huh." Zach looked totally unimpressed. He crossed his arms in front of his chest and didn't crack a smile for the next fifteen minutes. Mary Anne couldn't imagine why he had bothered to show up.

The moment the play was over (to wild applause) Zach grabbed James by the arm. "Hey, how about some football?" he said.

"I don't know. I'm sort of busy right now," James began.

"C'mon. Ditch this baby stuff and let's toss around the pigskin," said Zach, and James looked completely confused.

Zach pulled James down the driveway. Mary Anne didn't know why James let himself be dragged along, or why he didn't speak up. A lot of kids wanted to talk to him about the play, and James was letting Zach ruin his big moment for him. It didn't make sense.

Then Mary Anne thought about Dawn and Travis and got an idea. Dawn would be sure to read the notebook. Maybe this was Mary Anne's chance to tell her some things she'd been thinking about.

Tuesday (con't)
Even though the play
went well, I can't
stop thinking about
James and the way

he let himself be controlled by Zach. I hate to say it, Dawn, but it made me think of you and Travis. Zach is trying to make James into something Zach wants him to be, and, well, can you see that Travis is doing the same thing with you? You know I'm not saying this to hurt your feelings, but it's something you should really think about. Travis is trying to make you over into someone you don't want to be. You're great, just the way you are. Please don't let him change you, and don't hang around anymore waiting for him to drop by. That's not your style. Kristy, I hope you're not angry

with me for writing
this in the club note-
book, and Dawn, I
hope you're not angry,
period. But it's easier
for me to write this
than to say it. I hope
you understand. And
I hope you'll see Lewis
when he comes to town.

You're probably wondering why I would even *want* to see Travis again after that scene in the park. After all, I had seen him kissing another girl, so what could be left between us? I was tempted to forget the whole thing (and Travis, too) but I couldn't. I wanted Travis to know that I was on to him, and there was only one way I could do that. I'd have to wait until he left school with the girl and follow them again. But this time would be different. This time, I would confront Travis!

What did I hope to accomplish? Well, if nothing else, I would *embarrass* him! I could just picture how Travis would react when I bumped into him with his girlfriend. Let's see how cool and confident he'd be then!

I got my chance the following Tuesday afternoon. We had a quiz at the end of the day, and our teacher said we could leave as soon as we handed in our papers. What a lucky break! I whizzed through the test, double-checked my answers (it was a multiple-choice test), and left school fifteen minutes early. I had plenty of time to catch Travis as he left SHS.

My heart was pounding as I waited on a bench near the front steps of the school. I was wearing sunglasses, and I kept my head ducked down. I wanted to make sure that I spotted Travis before he recognized me!

Soon the bell rang, and kids came pouring out of the double doors. I saw Travis and caught my breath. He was alone! My mind raced with possibilities. Maybe he had broken up with the girl. Maybe he realized *I* was the girl he had wanted all along. Maybe the two of us could spend a wonderful afternoon together. Maybe, maybe, maybe . . .

There I was, lost in fantasyland when Sara (Kristy had found out her name for me) appeared on the scene. She darted up to Travis, and he grabbed her in a big bear hug. They hurried down the steps, just inches away from me. (I didn't need the sunglasses after all, because they never even looked at me. They were too wrapped up in each other.) My heart sank, but I was more determined than ever.

It was time to catch Travis in a trap.

I decided the best place to "bump into" them would be downtown. That way I could pretend that I was out shopping. (I certainly didn't want Travis to know that I had waited for him outside his school.)

Travis and Sara walked briskly along, and I kept a half block behind them. I didn't feel nervous at all because I was absolutely sure I was doing the right thing. The only question now was, where should I run into them?

I got my chance outside the Merry-Go-Round. It was a bright, sunny day, and the Merry-Go-Round was holding a sidewalk sale. Customers were jamming the area in front of the store, looking for bargains, and Travis and Sara had stopped in front of a display rack.

Travis was pointing to a pair of gold hoop earrings, when I positioned myself on the opposite side of the rack. If I waited a few more seconds, he'd be bound to see me. The moment he gave the rack a little spin, we'd be staring right into each other's eyes!

"I really like the silver hoops better," Sara was saying. I remember thinking what a wispy little-girl voice she had, and then it happened. The rack shifted and Travis and I were face-to-face. The moment of truth at last!

I gave him a casual smile, and to my amazement, he *grinned* back at me. "Hi, Dawn," he said in a friendly way. He didn't sound the least bit embarrassed! I was baffled, but I tried to be cool.

"Hi, Travis. I guess this is one of your favorite spots." I figured he deserved a little dig. After all, he had taken *me* to the Merry-Go-Round not too long ago, and now he was back in the same spot (with another girl).

He laughed, totally missing the point. "It sure looks that way, doesn't it?" Sara, who had been paying no attention to the conversation, suddenly held up a pair of heavy gold hoop earrings.

"What do you think, Travis?" she asked, ignoring me. "Are these too big?"

I couldn't resist. "Yes, definitely too big. They look like they should be holding up a shower curtain."

Sara frowned and gave Travis a "who-is-this-person?" look, and he introduced us.

"Dawn is from California, too," he added.

"Really?" Sara gave me a cool smile. "Oh, now I remember," she said, as if a light bulb had switched on inside her head. "Dawn Schafer . . . the little girl you told me about."

Little girl? I was steaming. What nerve. I

needed a really stinging comeback, but my mind was a blank. And the next words out of Sara's mouth were even worse. "I'm sure you've turned her into a real beauty, Travis," she murmured.

That did it! "I was already a beauty," I said hotly. I suppose it was a very conceited thing to say, but I didn't care.

Sara and Travis exchanged an amused look. I have *never* been so embarrassed in my life, and I knew I was making a fool out of myself. The only thing to do was get out of there — fast.

"I have to get home," I muttered.

"Nice to have met you," Sara said. She looked like she was going to burst out laughing the minute my back was turned.

"See you around." Travis grinned at me as if nothing had changed. How could he be so casual when my whole world had turned upside down?

I practically ran all the way home. I felt hurt, angry, upset, and *very* foolish. I didn't say two words during dinner and bounded upstairs to my room the minute the dishes were done.

"You're pretty quiet," Mary Anne said. She had come into my room so softly, I hadn't heard her. I was sprawled on my bed, math book in hand, but my mind was on Travis and Sara.

"I'm thinking," I told her. I looked at her and then looked away.

She sat down at my desk, watching me. "Did you ever see *My Fair Lady*?" she asked. "You know, the movie based on the play *Pygmalion*?"

What was she getting at? I sat up in bed, scrunching a pillow behind my head. "I saw it a long time ago. We rented it once."

Mary Anne looked pleased. "Then I guess you remember the story. You know how proper Professor Higgins turns Eliza Doolittle, the Cockney girl, into his 'fair lady'?"

"Sure. He changed everything about her, the way she walked and talked and even the way she dressed. He wanted to make her into a real lady."

Mary Anne stared at me. "Well," she said slowly, "I never liked that."

I nodded. "Me, neither. Eliza should have been allowed to be herself."

"Exactly."

We were both very quiet, and then it hit me. "I get it," I said. "You're talking about Travis and me." Mary Anne didn't answer, and I thought about it a little more. "He wanted to change me and make me into someone else." I hesitated. "But why did he choose *me*? There were dozens of girls he could have picked."

"Who knows? I think he really liked you at first. Or maybe he was interested because you were from California."

I sighed. Everything was falling into place. Travis had never liked me as much as I had liked him. I was simply a "project" for him. I felt a *little* better, having figured out what was going on, but now I had another problem. What should I do next?

Mary Anne must have read my mind. "I think you should confront him," she said. "Tell him exactly what you think."

"I think so, too. It won't be easy. That's what I thought I was going to do today. But I know it's the right thing to do." I smiled at her. "You've been a big help, Mary Anne."

"I'm glad." She hugged me and headed toward the door. "Oh, and Dawn, there's one more thing you need to do."

"What's that?"

She grinned. "Be sure you read the club notebook."

Now that I had made up my mind what to do, I didn't stop to think twice. I didn't make elaborate plans to follow Travis, or think about what I was going to say to him. I just reached for the phone, hoping that the right words would come to me. (Sometimes when you have to do something really hard, it's better not to plan too much.)

"Dawn, how are you?" exclaimed Travis when he picked up the phone.

He acted like nothing was wrong! His voice was so warm and friendly, I almost lost my cool, but I knew I had to be strong.

"I'm fine," I told him. "In fact, I've always been fine, but it took me awhile to figure that out."

"Huh?"

I took a deep breath. "You don't get it, do

you?" I rushed on. "Well, maybe I can explain it to you."

"Okay, shoot." A tiny note of doubt crept into his voice.

I braced myself for the toughest part of all. "You really hurt me, Travis."

"I *hurt* you?" He sounded incredulous.

"Yes, you did. You told me how to dress, how to fix my hair, how to act. You tried to make me into something I'm not."

There was a long pause. "You're right. I don't get it," he said finally. "How could something like that hurt you? You're a great-looking girl, Dawn. I just figured you could use a few suggestions on how to dress and do your hair."

"It was more than a few, but anyway, that's not the point. You can't imagine what a big effect you had on me. I took everything you said to heart." I hesitated, twisting the phone cord around my fingers. "Maybe you can't understand this, Travis, but I practically ran in circles trying to please you. I tried so hard to be everything you wanted me to be." It's funny, but even as I said the words, I realized that the harder I tried, the more hopeless things had become. I knew now that I could *never* be what Travis wanted (and that I didn't want to be).

Travis gave a little laugh. "Dawn, I really think you're making too much of this. You know, if we could just get together and talk this over, I think you'd see things my way."

"I don't think so," I said quietly.

"You mean you don't want to see me just because I told you to wear combs in your hair? I can't believe it."

"It's a lot more than that, Travis. Look, I'll give you the perfect example. Remember when you wanted me to get that third hole punched in my ear? I actually felt guilty because I didn't want to go along with it. I'm just glad I had the brains not to listen to you."

"Dawn, you're making a big deal out of nothing," Travis sputtered. Now he was beginning to sound *really* uncomfortable.

"No, it's true. You've been trying to make me over ever since the day you met me," I said, cutting him off. "You wanted to change everything about me. I just didn't see it in the beginning."

"Dawn, this is crazy."

"It's not crazy at all," I said smoothly. "I've had time to think about it, and I've talked things over with Mary Anne. You never liked me for myself, just for what you could make me into. It all makes sense now."

"Look, I never wanted to hurt you, Dawn — "

"Maybe not, but that's what happened. Besides everything else, you led me on. You let me think I was special to you, but you were seeing Sara at the same time." I felt very calm. "Anyway, I think we should just say good-bye now."

"Say good-bye? Are you serious?"

"Very serious," I said softly. "That's why I called you tonight, Travis. To say good-bye, and to say that I hope you find the perfect girl for you. She's probably out there somewhere, Travis, but I'm not her. Maybe it's Sara."

Travis started to say something, but I didn't give him a chance. I hung up the receiver very gently and stared out the window for a few minutes.

It was over. And I knew I had done the right thing.

The reaction at the next BSC meeting was just what I had hoped for.

"Dawn! I can't believe you did it. I'm so

proud of you!" Claudia was beaming. "He really got what was coming to him."

"Travis must have been furious," Stacey chimed in. "I wish I could have been there."

"I'm just happy you're rid of him," Mary Anne said. "You finally caught on."

"It took a little help from my friends," I added. "For awhile, I thought there was something wrong with *me*."

"Ha! That's probably what he wanted you to think," Kristy said. She tilted her visor back. "I had no idea Travis was such a jerk. He hangs around with my brothers all the time."

Mary Anne looked up from the notebook. "Well, he's probably okay when he's with guys because he's not trying to make them over."

Kristy nodded. "I guess you're right. The main thing is that he's out of Dawn's life for good — " I started to giggle, and Kristy stopped in mid-sentence. "What's so funny?"

"I just thought of something I should have said. I should have told Travis to have his hair trimmed and to get rid of those stone-washed jeans. He could use a few fashion tips himself!"

"You would have been wasting your

breath," Stacey said, examining her nail polish. "He's so conceited, he probably thinks he's perfect."

I was struggling with a math problem later that night when Mary Anne came into my room. She looked a little embarrassed, and I wondered why.

"How's it going?" She glanced at my math book, but I knew she had something else on her mind.

"Okay." I closed the book and spun around in my seat. "I can take a break if you want to talk."

"Well . . . sure," Mary Anne said, settling herself on the bed. I waited while she fumbled in her pocket for a white envelope. "I . . . just wanted to tell you again that I'm really proud of the way you handled Travis."

I smiled at her. "I'm glad. But I bet that isn't why you came in here."

Mary Anne flushed. "Well, I — Okay, I'll be honest with you. I've got something for you." She glanced at the envelope but drew back when I reached for it. "No, wait! Before you read it, I want to explain something."

From the look on Mary Anne's face, I knew it must be something important. And I knew there was no way I could rush Mary Anne. She would tell me in her own good time.

"Do you remember when I told you about Lewis?"

"Lewis?" I drew a blank, and then it hit me. "Oh, yeah. Logan's cousin. What about him?"

"Well, guess what? His visit to Stoneybrook is all planned!"

"Really?" I know Mary Anne expected me to look thrilled, but I just couldn't. My hand edged back to the math book. I had about a million problems to work on, and Mary Anne was all set for a long conversation about some guy I didn't even know!

"Don't you get it?" she said finally. "Lewis wants to meet you."

"That's crazy," I said, sharpening a new pencil. "He doesn't even know me."

Mary Anne cleared her throat. "That's not exactly true. He, um, knows a *little* bit about you."

"How could he?" I was flipping through the book, trying to find my place when I paused and said, "Mary Anne, what have you done?"

She was blushing all the way up to her hair roots. "Now don't get mad, Dawn, but Logan and I told Lewis a few things about you. And I sent him your picture."

"What?!"

"Please don't get upset. If you just think about it, you'll realize it was a great idea. Logan says Lewis is a really neat guy, and I think he's just what you need now." She was still clutching the white envelope and she handed it to me.

"It's a letter addressed to me," I said, turning it over. "Mary Anne, what's going on?"

"It's from Lewis. Isn't that great? He must have liked your picture and the things Logan and I told him, so he decided to write to you. I *said* he was a great guy."

"Terrific," I muttered, tearing open the envelope. I scanned the first few lines and relaxed a little. Lewis said he had heard a lot about me, and he wanted to meet me. He also said I was very pretty and that we had a lot in common. He didn't sound so bad, but I just wasn't interested in meeting another boy at the moment. Why couldn't Mary Anne figure that out?

"Well?" Mary Anne said. She stood next to me, trying to read over my shoulder. "What do you think?"

I shrugged. "He seems like a pretty nice guy." A picture of a boy with dark brown hair and a great smile fell out of the envelope. "And he's even good-looking."

"Definitely. And he's a lot of fun, too. That's why Logan and I want this to work out." She looked at me very seriously. "You'll see him when he visits, won't you? *Please*, Dawn."

I looked at the picture again. I didn't feel any sparks the way I had with Travis, but Lewis *did* seem nice. Still, the timing was wrong, all wrong.

"Well?" Mary Anne said impatiently. "Will you see him or won't you?"

I sighed. "I don't know."

"Dawn, puh-*leeze!*"

"Okay, okay. If Lewis wants to take me out when he comes to Stoneybrook, I'll go. I guess."

"Good!" said Mary Anne. "That's all I wanted to hear."

Later, when I was alone in my room, I read Lewis's letter again. (Okay, I'll tell you the truth. I read it *three* more times.) I'm not sure exactly what I was looking for, but I wondered if Lewis was too good to be true. He seemed funny, smart, not at all stuck-up, and *nice*. I'll show you what I mean. He started out by describing himself. (We had to do this once in English class, and it was the toughest assignment I've ever had.)

DEAR DAWN,

I KNOW LOGAN IS GOING TO MAKE ME SOUND LIKE SOME MOVIE STAR, SO I THOUGHT I'D SEND YOU MY PICTURE. THIS WAY YOU CAN MAKE UP YOUR OWN MIND. I'M FIVE TEN, AND I HAVE BROWN EYES AND BROWN HAIR. NO MATTER WHAT LOGAN TELLS YOU, GIRLS DO NOT FAINT AT MY FEET!

WAIT, I TAKE THAT BACK. A GIRL DID FAINT AT MY FEET ONCE. HER NAME WAS JENNY O'CONNOR. WE WERE DOING A SCENE FROM A PLAY CALLED THE GLASS MENAGERIE AND JENNY HAD THE WORST CASE OF STAGE FRIGHT I'VE EVER SEEN. THE CURTAIN WENT UP AND SHE PASSED OUT COLD!

SO MUCH FOR A BIG OPENING NIGHT. I THOUGHT YOU MIGHT BE INTERESTED IN ACTING, SINCE YOU'RE FROM THE WEST COAST. WHENEVER I THINK OF CALIFORNIA, I THINK OF MOVIE STARS AND HEALTH FOOD. BUT I COULD BE WRONG. WHEN I TELL PEOPLE THAT I'M FROM LOUISVILLE, THEY ALWAYS THINK THAT I LOVE GRITS (YECCH!) AND THAT I HAVE A HOUND DOG NAMED BEAU! (NEITHER IS TRUE.)

WELL, I BETTER WIND THINGS UP HERE. I HOPE I HEAR FROM YOU!

'BYE FOR NOW.
LEWIS

Did I write him back? Yes. But I took my time, and I decided to be very casual.

Dear Lewis,
It was really nice to hear from you. I can't believe that

Logan and Mary Anne sent you my picture! But you know what? I'm glad they did, because now we've met each other. (Sort of.)

I thought I'd start by telling you a little bit about myself. First of all, I love California, but not because it's full of movie stars. In fact I've never even met a movie star, even though a couple of them live near my dad.

You mentioned health food—I love it! Mom and I are always trying out new vegetarian recipes. (Don't gag. Spinach pie is delicious.)

Am I an actress? No way! People have always told me I should go into modeling or acting, but I know I'd get stage fright, just like your friend Jenny.

I'd like to tell you a little about Stoneybrook, but I have a math test tomorrow

(panic time!) so I better go.
'Bye for now.
Dawn

I read my letter to Lewis twice before sealing the envelope. I wondered if I could have made it more interesting, decided that I couldn't, and finally dropped it in the mailbox. Imagine how surprised I was when I got a letter back four days later! Lewis must have written the minute he received my letter.

DEAR DAWN,

THIS WILL HAVE TO BE SHORT, AS I HAVE A MATH TEST, TOO. MATH ISN'T MY BEST SUBJECT (ENGLISH IS) SO I HAVE TO STUDY EXTRA HARD. I'VE DONE ALL THE PROBLEMS IN THE BOOK THREE TIMES, SO UNLESS I TOTALLY FREAK OUT DURING THE TEST I'LL BE OKAY.

I LIKED HEARING ABOUT CALIFORNIA. I GUESSED THAT YOU WERE INTO HEALTH FOODS (ONE RIGHT ANSWER) AND THAT YOU WANTED TO BE AN ACTRESS (ONE WRONG ANSWER.) THAT GIVES ME A

SCORE OF FIFTY. LET'S HOPE I DO BETTER ON THE TEST TOMORROW.

GUESS IT'S TIME TO HIT THE BOOKS. I'M WONDERING WHAT KIND OF THINGS WE CAN DO IN STONEYBROOK. A MOVIE? A CONCERT? A WALK IN THE PARK?

STAY IN TOUCH. YOUR PAL,

LEWIS

It sounded like Lewis was planning to spend a lot of time with me when he visited Logan. Would it be just the two of us, or would we be doing things with Logan and Mary Anne? I decided I didn't really want to see him alone. That would be too much like a "date." But if he wanted to be friends, that would be okay.

Dear Lewis,

I figured out what to do when you visit Logan. How about a tour of Stoneybrook? I bet you've never seen a small New England town. What do we do for fun? We've got movies and there's a big shopping mall, but you have to drive to get to it. And of course we have pizza parlors. Do you know I found a place that sells vegetarian pizza? It has stir-fried snow peas and broccoli on it, and it's great!

Your friend,
Dawn

In return, Lewis sent me a postcard of Louisville, Kentucky. The picture was of a beautiful boat called *The Belle of Louisville*, and this was the message:

HI, DAWN,

YOU'RE KIDDING ABOUT THE BROCCOLI PIZZA, RIGHT? (PLEASE SAY YOU ARE!) I LIKE TO TRY NEW THINGS, BUT THAT'S PUSHING IT A LITTLE. STILL, IF YOU SAY IT'S GOOD, I'LL TAKE YOUR WORD FOR IT. I'LL SEE YOU IN STONEYBROOK SOON. I CAN'T WAIT TO MEET YOU. I'M REALLY LOOKING FORWARD TO IT.

'BYE, LEWIS

He was looking forward to coming to Stoneybrook. He was looking forward to seeing me. I read the postcard at least half a dozen times and put it in my notebook.

Mary Anne teased me just a little that night when I tucked the postcard into the mirror over my dresser.

"So you're changing your mind a little about Lewis?"

"He sounds . . . interesting," I said with a smile.

"Just interesting?"

"Okay, he sounds pretty terrific." I paused. "But I don't want to get my hopes up too much. Remember how crazy I was over Travis?"

"Lewis is different," Mary Anne said firmly. "Can't you tell from his letters?"

I shrugged. "He seems different. He seems nice. And I don't think he wants to change me. We'll probably like each other. Just as friends," I added quickly.

"That's what I'm hoping for." Mary Anne sighed happily and flopped onto my bed. "I want you and Lewis to be great friends. Or maybe even something more," she said with a twinkle in her eye.

"Just friends will be fine."

Mary Anne giggled. "Only time will tell."

About the Author

ANN M. MARTIN did *a lot* of baby-sitting when she was growing up in Princeton, New Jersey. Now her favorite baby-sitting charge is her cat, Mouse, who lives with her in her Manhattan apartment.

Ann Martin's Apple Paperbacks include *Yours Turly, Shirley*; *Ten Kids, No Pets*; *With You and Without You*; *Bummer Summer*; and all the other books in the Baby-sitters Club series.

She is a former editor of books for children, and was graduated from Smith College. She likes ice cream, the beach, and *I Love Lucy*; and she hates to cook.

Look for #38

KRISTY'S MYSTERY ADMIRER

Shannon pulled the envelope out of the pocket of her school uniform and handed it to me. I was so excited I could hardly breathe. Then I realized that David Michael was at my elbow.

"Let's go to my room," I said hastily. Shannon and I thundered up the stairs. David Michael was at our heels.

When we reached the door to my room and I realized that we were still a trio, I had to say, "David Michael, this is private. You can't come in." (I couldn't help being blunt. I was nearing hysteria.)

"But I want to know what's going on," he said.

"Maybe I'll tell you later," I replied "*Maybe.* Anyway, this is girl stuff." I knew that would get him.

"*Girl* stuff! Gross. Forget it. I don't want to know after all."

I grinned at Shannon. David Michael had taken off like a shot.

Shannon and I darted into my room and I closed the door behind us. We flopped on my bed, and I let the envelope dangle between my thumb and forefinger.

Then we examined the envelope together. The front said simply KRISTY. The word was typed but the "I" had been dotted with a tiny heart sticker. A flower sticker had been placed carefully in each corner of the envelope.

"Maybe it's not for me," I said. "It doesn't say 'Kristy Thomas.' It just says 'Kristy.' "

"Well, there aren't any Kristys at my house," Shannon replied. "And I can't think of any other Kristys in the neighborhood — and I know practically everyone around here."

I turned the envelope over. On the back were more hearts and flowers. All I could do was stare at the envelope.

"Well, open it before I die!" cried Shannon.

I ripped the envelope open.

Read all the books
in the Baby-sitters Club series
by Ann M. Martin

1 *Kristy's Great Idea*
Kristy's great idea is to start *The Baby-sitters Club*!

2 *Claudia and the Phantom Phone Calls*
Someone mysterious is calling Claudia!

3 *The Truth About Stacey*
Stacey's different . . . and it's harder on her than anyone knows.

4 *Mary Anne Saves the Day*
Mary Anne is tired of being treated like a baby. It's time to take charge!

5 *Dawn and the Impossible Three*
Dawn thought she'd be baby-sitting — not *monster*-sitting!

6 *Kristy's Big Day*
Kristy's a baby-sitter — and a bridesmaid, too!

7 *Claudia and Mean Janine*
Claudia's big sister is super smart . . . and super *mean*.

8 *Boy-Crazy Stacey*
Stacey's too busy being *boy-crazy* to baby-sit!

9 *The Ghost at Dawn's House*
Creaking stairs, a secret passage — there must be a ghost at Dawn's house!

#10 *Logan Likes Mary Anne!*
Mary Anne has a crush on a *boy* baby-sitter!

#11 *Kristy and the Snobs*
The kids in Kristy's new neighborhood are S-N-O-B-S!

#12 *Claudia and the New Girl*
Claudia might give up the club — and it's all Ashley's fault!

#13 *Good-bye Stacey, Good-bye*
Oh, no! Stacey McGill is moving back to New York!

#14 *Hello, Mallory*
Is Mallory Pike good enough to join the club?

#15 *Little Miss Stoneybrook . . . and Dawn*
Everyone in Stoneybrook has gone beauty-pageant crazy!

#16 *Jessi's Secret Language*
Jessi's new charge is teaching her a *secret language*.

#17 *Mary Anne's Bad-Luck Mystery*
Will Mary Anne's bad luck ever go away?

#18 *Stacey's Mistake*
Has Stacey made a big mistake by inviting the Baby-sitters to New York City?

#19 *Claudia and the Bad Joke*
Claudia is headed for trouble when she baby-sits for a practical joker.

#20 *Kristy and the Walking Disaster*
Can Kristy's Krushers beat Bart's Bashers?

#21 *Mallory and the Trouble With Twins*
Sitting for the Arnold twins is double trouble!

#22 *Jessi Ramsey, Pet-sitter*
Jessi has to baby-sit for a house full of . . . *pets!*

#23 *Dawn on the Coast*
Could Dawn be a California girl for good?

#24 *Kristy and the Mother's Day Surprise*
There are all *kinds* of surprises this Mother's Day.

#25 *Mary Anne and the Search for Tigger*
Tigger is missing! Has he been catnapped?

#26 *Claudia and the Sad Good-bye*
Claudia never thought she'd have to say good-bye to her grandmother.

#27 *Jessi and the Superbrat*
Jessi gets to baby-sit for a TV star!

#28 *Welcome Back, Stacey!*
Stacey's moving again . . . back to Stoneybrook!

#29 *Mallory and the Mystery Diary*
Only Mal can solve the mystery in the old diary.

#30 *Mary Anne and the Great Romance*
Mary Anne's father and Dawn's mother are getting *married!*

#31 *Dawn's Wicked Stepsister*
Dawn thought having a stepsister was going to be fun. Was she ever wrong!

#32 *Kristy and the Secret of Susan*
Even Kristy can't learn all of Susan's secrets.

#33 *Claudia and the Great Search*
There are *no* baby pictures of Claudia. Could she have been . . . adopted?!

#34 *Mary Anne and Too Many Boys*
Will a summer romance come between Mary Anne and Logan?

#35 *Stacey and the Mystery of Stoneybrook*
Stacey discovers a *haunted house* in Stoneybrook!

#36 *Jessi's Baby-sitter*
How could Jessi's parents have gotten a *baby-sitter* for her?

#37 *Dawn and the Older Boy*
Will Dawn's heart be broken by an older boy?

#38 *Kristy's Mystery Admirer*
Someone is sending Kristy *love notes!*

Super Specials:

1 *Baby-sitters on Board!*
Guess who's going on a dream vacation? The Baby-sitters!

2 *Baby-sitters' Summer Vacation*
Good-bye, Stoneybrook . . . hello, Camp Mohawk!

3 *Baby-sitters' Winter Vacation*
The Baby-sitters are off for a week of winter fun!

4 *Baby-sitters' Island Adventure*
Two of the Baby-sitters are shipwrecked!

by Ann M. Martin

The Baby-sitters' business is booming! And that gets Stacey, Kristy, Claudia, and the rest of The Baby-sitters Club members in all kinds of adventures...at school, with boys, and, of course, baby-sitting!

Something new and exciting happens in every Baby-sitters Club book. Collect and read them all!

❑	MG43388-1	#1	Kristy's Great Idea	$2.95
❑	MG43513-2	#2	Claudia and the Phantom Phone Calls	$2.95
❑	MG43511-6	#3	The Truth About Stacey	$2.95
❑	MG43512-4	#4	Mary Anne Saves the Day	$2.95
❑	MG43720-8	#5	Dawn and the Impossible Three	$2.95
❑	MG43899-9	#6	Kristy's Big Day	$2.95
❑	MG43719-4	#7	Claudia and Mean Janine	$2.95
❑	MG43509-4	#8	Boy-Crazy Stacey	$2.95
❑	MG43508-6	#9	The Ghost at Dawn's House	$2.95
❑	MG43387-3	#10	Logan Likes Mary Anne!	$2.95
❑	MG43660-0	#11	Kristy and the Snobs	$2.95
❑	MG43721-6	#12	Claudia and the New Girl	$2.95
❑	MG41127-6	#13	Good-bye Stacey, Good-bye	$2.95
❑	MG41128-4	#14	Hello, Mallory	$2.95
❑	MG43717-8	#15	Little Miss Stoneybrook...and Dawn	$2.95
❑	MG41586-7	#16	Jessi's Secret Language	$2.75
❑	MG43659-7	#17	Mary Anne's Bad Luck Mystery	$2.95
❑	MG48718-6	#18	Stacey's Mistake	$2.95
❑	MG43510-8	#19	Claudia and the Bad Joke	$2.95
❑	MG43722-4	#20	Kristy and the Walking Disaster	$2.95
❑	MG43507-8	#21	Mallory and the Trouble With Twins	$2.95
❑	MG43658-9	#22	Jessi Ramsey, Pet-sitter	$2.95
❑	MG43900-5	#23	Dawn on the Coast	$2.95
❑	MG43506-X	#24	Kristy and the Mother's Day Surprise	$2.95
❑	MG43347-4	#25	Mary Anne and the Search for Tiger	$2.95
❑	MG42503-X	#26	Claudia and the Sad Good-bye	$2.95
❑	MG42502-1	#27	Jessi and the Superbrat	$2.95

More titles...

titles continued...

❑	MG42501-3	#28	Welcome Back, Stacey!	$2.95
❑	MG42500-5	#29	Mallory and the Mystery Diary	$2.95
❑	MG42498-X	#30	Mary Anne and the Great Romance	$2.95
❑	MG42497-1	#31	Dawn's Wicked Stepsister	$2.95
❑	MG42496-3	#32	Kristy and the Secret of Susan	$2.95
❑	MG42495-5	#33	Claudia and the Great Search	$2.95
❑	MG42494-7	#34	Mary Anne and Too Many Boys	$2.95
❑	MG42508-0	#35	Stacey and the Mystery of Stoneybrook	$2.95
❑	MG43565-5	#36	Jessi's Baby-sitter	$2.95
❑	MG43566-3	#37	Dawn and the Older Boy	$2.95
❑	MG43567-1	#38	Kristy's Mystery Admirer	$2.95
❑	MG41588-3		Baby-sitters on Board! Super Special #1	$2.95
❑	MG42419-X		Baby-sitters' Summer Vacation Super Special #2	$2.95
❑	MG42499-8		Baby-sitters' Winter Vacation Super Special #3	$3.50
❑	MG42493-9		Baby-sitters' Island Adventure Super Special #4	$3.50
❑	MG43745-3		The Baby-sitters Club 1990-91 Student Planner and Date Book	$7.95
❑	MG43744-5		The Baby-sitters Club 1991 Calendar	$8.95
❑	MG43803-4		The Baby-sitters Club Notebook	$1.95

Available wherever you buy books...or use this order form.

Scholastic Inc., P.O. Box 7502, 2931 E. McCarty Street, Jefferson City, MO 65102

Please send me the books I have checked above. I am enclosing $_____
(please add $2.00 to cover shipping and handling). Send check or money order — no cash or C.O.D.s please.

Name _____

Address _____

City _____ State/Zip _____

Please allow four to six weeks for delivery. Offer good in the U.S. only. Sorry, mail orders are not available to residents of Canada. Prices subject to change.

BSC390

NOW

THE BABY-SITTERS CLUB®

IS A GAME!

- What would you do if you found your baby-sitting charges running around the neighborhood with their underwear on their heads?
- Who would you pick as the "cutest boy" in your school?
- Would you dare to lie on your stomach and tie your shoe—in front of everyone?

Now you, too, can be like Kristy, Stacey and Claudia when you play the official Baby-sitters Club Game. Try to rack up the most points as you answer questions about baby-sitting, boys and best friends. There's even trivia from the Baby-sitters Club books plus silly stunts to do, too! Just roll the dice, pick a card and the fun begins! Perfect for sleep-overs, parties and after school!

YOU'LL FIND THIS
GREAT MILTON BRADLEY GAME
AT TOY STORES AND BOOKSTORES
NEAR YOU!

It's finally here...

T-SHIRT!

The First Official T-Shirt for all Baby-sitters Club Fans!

Show everyone you're a fan of the best club in the world — The Baby-sitters Club!

This awesome T-shirt is:

★ 100% cotton!
★ Has the official Baby-sitters Club logo!
★ One size fits all!

Wear the T-shirt everyone will want! Just fill in the coupon below and mail it with your payment today!

Allow 6–8 weeks for delivery.

❑ YES! Please send me____ Baby-sitters Club T-shirt(s) — 28148-9 — at $8.95 plus $2.00 shipping and handling (a total of $10.95) for each T-shirt ordered. I've enclosed my check or money order (no cash please) for $_____, made payable to: Scholastic Inc.

Name _____ Age _____

Address _____

City _____ State _____ Zip _____

Fill in and mail coupon with your payment to: Baby-sitters Club T-Shirt, Scholastic Inc., P.O. Box 7500, 2931 E. McCarty St., Jefferson City, MO 65102.

BST1189

WIN A TRIP TO NEW YORK CITY!

Enter THE BABY-SITTERS CLUB® *Adventure Giveaway*

"Where are the Baby-sitters going on their next Super Special Adventure?"

Guess the right place and win the trip of your dreams! We'll send the Grand Prize Winner of this Giveaway and his/her parent or guardian on an all-expense paid weekend (2 nights, 3 days) to New York City! Just fill in the coupon below and return by November 30, 1990.

500 Second Prize Winners get Baby-sitters Club Sun Visors!

Hint:
The Baby-sitters will need their sun visors on their next Super Special adventure!

Rules: Entries must be postmarked by November 30, 1990. Winners will be picked at random and notified by mail. No purchase necessary. Valid only in the U.S. Void where prohibited. Taxes on prizes are the responsibility of the winners and their immediate families. Employees of Scholastic Inc.; its agencies, affiliates, subsidiaries; and their immediate families not eligible. For a complete list of winners, send a self-addressed stamped envelope to The Baby-sitters Club Adventure Giveaway, Giveaway Winners List, at the address provided below.

Fill in the coupon below or write the information on a 3" x 5" piece of paper and mail to: **THE BABY-SITTERS CLUB ADVENTURE GIVEAWAY**, Scholastic Inc., P.O. Box 1068, Jefferson City, MO 65102.

The Baby-sitters Club Adventure Giveaway

The Baby-sitters' next Super Special Adventure will be in: _____

_____

Name_____ Age_____

Street_____

City_____ State_____ Zip_____

Where did you buy this *Baby-sitters Club* book?

❑ Bookstore ❑ Drugstore ❑ Supermarket ❑ Library

❑ Book Club ❑ Book Fair ❑ Other_____(specify)

BSC190

Take the Baby-sitters to School with You!

1990-91 School Planner and Date Book!

by Ann M. Martin

Make your school year the best ever with **The Baby-sitters Club 1990-91 School Planner and Date Book!** It has 148 pages of EVERYTHING you need and more! You get:

- ☆ Full-page calendars for each month of the school year!
- ☆ Weekly spreads with space for school assignments, after-school activities, and baby-sitting jobs!
- ☆ 18 fill-in pages for phone numbers, addresses, birthdays, school information and more!
- ☆ Weekly diary pages for personal notes!
- ☆ Baby-sitters Club tips, trivia, and messages throughout!
- ☆ Monthly baby-sitting pages for important notes on clients, earnings, and special reminders!
- ☆ Full-page yearly calendars for 1990 and 1991!

Available wherever you buy Baby-sitters Club books!

Planner is 8 1/2" x 11."

BSC190

More books you will love by . . .

APPLE® PAPERBACKS

ANN M. MARTIN

author of your favorite series

THE BABY-SITTERS CLUB®

Don't miss any of these great Apple® Paperbacks

❑	MW43622-8	Bummer Summer	$2.75
❑	MW43621-X	Inside Out	$2.75
❑	MW43618-X	Me and Katie (the Pest)	$2.75
❑	MW43619-8	Stage Fright	$2.75
❑	MW43620-1	Ten Kids, No Pets	$2.75
❑	MW43625-2	With You and Without You	$2.75
❑	MW42809-8	Yours Turly, Shirley	$2.75

Available wherever you buy books . . .
or use coupon below.

Scholastic Inc. P.O. Box 7502, 2932 E. McCarty Street, Jefferson City, MO 65102

Please send me the books I have checked above. I am enclosing $_____
(please add $2.00 to cover shipping and handling). Send check or money order—no cash or C.O.D.'s please.

Name _____

Address _____

City _____ State/Zip _____

Please allow four to six weeks for delivery. Offer good in U.S.A. only. Sorry, mail order not available to residents of Canada. Prices subject to change.

AM989